Ghost Detectives

THE MISSING DANCER

Emily Mason

PUFFIN

PUFFIN BOOKS

Published by the Penguin Group
Penguin Books Ltd, 80 Strand, London WC2R ORL, England
Penguin Group (USA) Inc., 375 Hudson Street, New York, New York 10014, USA
Penguin Group (Canada), 90 Eglinton Avenue East, Suite 700, Toronto, Ontario, Canada M4P 2Y3
(a division of Pearson Penguin Canada Inc.)
Penguin Ireland, 25 St Stephen's Green, Dublin 2, Ireland (a division of Penguin Books Ltd)
Penguin Group (Australia), 707 Collins Street, Melbourne, Victoria 3008, Australia
(a division of Pearson Australia Group Pty Ltd)
Penguin Books India Pvt Ltd, 11 Community Centre, Panchsheel Park, New Delhi – 110 017, India
Penguin Group (NZ), 67 Apollo Drive, Rosedale, Auckland 0632, New Zealand
(a division of Pearson New Zealand Ltd)
Penguin Books (South Africa) (Pty) Ltd, Block D, Rosebank Office Park, 181 Jan Smuts Avenue,
Parktown North, Gauteng 2193, South Africa

Penguin Books Ltd, Registered Offices: 80 Strand, London WC2R ORL, England

puffinbooks.com

First published 2013
002

Set in Baskerville MT Std 13/16 pt
Typeset by Palimpsest Book Production Limited, Falkirk, Stirlingshire
Printed in Great Britain by Clays Ltd, St Ives plc

British Library Cataloguing in Publication Data
A CIP catalogue record for this book is available from the British Library

ISBN: 978-0-141-34204-7

www.greenpenguin.co.uk

ALWAYS LEARNING   **PEARSON**

For my sister, Gayle Pierce

Contents

I

Reunions

Sarah glanced at her watch, then quickened her pace. She had arranged to meet Abi, Hannah and Grace early, so they could call in on their friend Simone before heading up to the museum. Her long red hair swished from side to side as she walked and her breath swirled into white mist in the cold air as she puffed out shapeless clouds, just like she used to do when she was little. She could feel it – today was going to be a good day.

It was Saturday morning, which meant the museum would open at ten and the ten volunteers – all from her school – had to be ready to get to work. The new town museum in the Grainger estate had only been open for three weeks, since the night of their big launch party at Hallowe'en, but already word of mouth had guaranteed them a busy day of guided tours every week. Sarah smiled to herself, thinking about how much she loved working as a museum volunteer. When she was at home nothing seemed to fit. Ever since her dad had moved out and got his own apartment, the house felt lopsided – all out of kilter. If she had to spend the whole weekend there, it would drive her completely crazy. The museum took up nearly the whole of Saturday and piano lessons and practice much of the rest, which meant Sarah could escape and that suited her just fine. It hurt her head to think about everything at home.

She rounded the final corner and there were the imposing black gates that announced the entrance to the driveway of the old Grainger house, which served as the museum. The house had been given to the town, along with most of its grounds, by Beryl and Audoen Grainger years ago. As Sarah drew closer she could see her three best friends leaning against the railings, deep in conversation. She stopped and watched them for a moment. Grace was telling one of her madcap stories by the look of it, and Abi and Hannah were hanging on her every word, smiling at her in a way only good friends do. As usual, Grace looked uber-cool: electric-blue pedal-pushers, her beloved pink Converse, an orange duffel coat and her hair in two plaits, tied at the end with hot-pink ribbons. Sarah spent her life in jeans, checked shirts and scuffed desert boots, but she loved her friend's quirky sense of style.

Hannah's long blonde hair looked freshly washed and glossy. Her tennis racket was parked on the ground at her feet – she must have practice later. Her nose was scrunched up as she anticipated the punchline of Grace's story, her eyes laughing before her mouth did. Sarah's new friend, Abi, looked happy. When she had first moved to the town that summer from America, she had seemed guarded and shy, but now she was a firm friend and Sarah couldn't imagine her not being part of the gang. She broke into a run and raced up to them.

'Morning, lazybones,' Grace sing-songed at her. 'What time do you call this?'

Sarah grinned at her. 'Delighted to see you too,' she joked.

'Finally!' Abi said, smiling warmly at her. 'Here we are, dying to see Simone again, and you make us wait, you diva. I can't believe how much I've missed Simone.'

Sarah arched her eyebrow. 'And you're *dying* to see her, Abi? Really?'

Abi stuck out her tongue playfully at her friend. 'You know what I mean,' she said.

Sarah grinned at her. 'You have to be careful what you say about undertakers, Abi,' she teased.

Simone Grainger lived in the gate lodge with her father and they ran the family funeral business from there. She had become friends with the girls since they had started volunteering at the museum. She was sixteen, only four years older than them, but she was home-schooled and worked as assistant undertaker to her father. That put her way ahead of Sarah and her friends in the cool stakes, as Grace liked to remind them. Sarah would never have imagined she'd end up being friends with an actual undertaker, but Simone wasn't like anyone else she'd ever met – and she was really glad they had all got to know each other.

It was Simone who had helped the girls when they'd made an amazing discovery up at the museum – a diary kept by Simone's grandmother, Beryl. In it they had read about a special ritual that had made Beryl a ghost detective, able to help ghosts who were haunted by their past lives. The diary had changed everything. Sarah, Abi, Hannah and Grace had done the ritual for a laugh, but then a ghost had turned up at the museum and it wasn't funny any more. Simone was the only one who knew their secret. Whenever they passed by, they dropped in at the gate lodge to see her and to fill her in on the latest instalment in their ghost stories.

'Come on, then,' Hannah said, picking up her racket and turning towards the open gate. 'Let's go see how our favourite undertaker is doing.'

They walked through the gate and on to the curving gravel driveway that led past the red-brick gate lodge. The neat plaque by the door announced it as: GRAINGER & SON & GRANDDAUGHTER, UNDERTAKERS AND FUNERAL PARLOUR. Hannah pressed the doorbell – it made no noise when you were outside, which always made visitors wonder if they had been heard – and they waited.

The heavy wooden door swung open suddenly and there stood Mr Grainger, Simone's dad, looking very solemn. When he realized it was the four girls, he smiled. 'Good morning, you lot,' he said, opening the door wide. 'Come in, come in. It's lovely to see you all again.'

'Hi, Mr Grainger,' Hannah said brightly. 'We just wanted to catch up with Simone before we go to the museum. Is she up?'

'She is, of course,' he said, ushering them into the large reception hall. 'Simone,' he called out, 'your delightful friends are here.'

Simone padded down the hallway, pulling her long dark hair into a ponytail as she walked. Her bare feet slapped gently on the wooden floor. She was wearing a ballet-length black skirt and a purple-and-black T-shirt. Sarah couldn't stop staring at her surprisingly dainty bare feet – it was so odd to see her out of her Doc Marten boots. Simone grinned at the four girls. 'Hello,' she called. 'Is the fire lit in the sitting room, Dad?'

'Yes, yes.' Mr Grainger nodded. 'First thing I did, cold morning like this. In you go and I'll bring in some tea.'

The girls filed into the cosy room behind Simone.

Sarah looked around and sighed happily. 'It's so nice to be here again,' she said, then added, 'and to see you again.' She knew she probably sounded a bit daft, but it was true. She'd missed their new friend while Simone had been away on holidays in France.

Simone smiled shyly at Sarah. 'I know,' she said, 'it's only two weeks, but it feels like an age since I've seen you all. I can't wait to hear everything.'

'No, you first,' Hannah said, settling herself into an armchair. 'How was the Grainger family reunion?'

Simone made a face. 'Same as every year – they all seem a bit madder, as far as I'm concerned, and I spend my time listening to stories about the "good old days"!'

'They have gatherings like that in America,' Abi said. 'You know, like, clan reunions for people who have Scottish or Irish ancestry, or whatever. We went to one when I was a kid.'

'I think we've got a bit of everything in our background,' Simone said with a smile. 'Or at least, that's what they like to claim.'

'And whereabouts in France did you all meet?' Abi asked. 'I'm so jealous, by the way – it would be awesome to see Europe.'

Simone got up to throw another log on the fire. 'In my great-uncle's chateau in Poitiers,' she said. 'It looks impressive from the outside, but it's a draughty old echoey place. I'm glad to be back home again,' she said, looking around appreciatively.

'Well, it wasn't the same without you here,' Grace said. 'Every time I went past, I couldn't help thinking that even the gate lodge was missing you – it seemed so empty.'

'Were people good enough not to die in your absence?' Sarah asked. She knew she was being mischievous, but Simone always took her teasing in her stride.

Simone looked over at Sarah and laughed. 'I've even missed that acerbic tongue of yours,' she joked. 'And, no, people didn't put off dying while we were gone, but Matthew and Harry handled things for the two weeks. You cheeky thing,' she added with a grin.

The door pushed open and Mr Grainger came in carrying a tray of tea and biscuits and five mugs. Grace jumped up to help him.

'Everything been running smoothly up at the old house?' he asked.

Hannah nodded. 'It's been great. Ever since the launch night we've been busy every Saturday. People seem to really enjoy the museum.'

'As well they might,' Mr Grainger said. 'All of you volunteers put such effort into it – it deserves to be a success. In fact, I was telling all the other Graingers about it and they are thrilled it's open again. They were very, very interested to hear the story about our Henry that you girls uncovered.'

Sarah, Abi, Hannah, Grace and Simone shared a smile. Mr Grainger only knew part of the story – he most definitely did not know about the ghost

7

of Louise-Anne Miller! She had arrived after the girls performed Beryl's ritual and she'd made life very interesting for a while, until they solved the mystery behind the letter she had received from her love, Henry Grainger, and she could at last rest in peace. Simone winked at Sarah.

'In fact,' Mr Grainger went on, 'I wouldn't be surprised if some of my relatives make their way over at some stage, to have a look.'

'Really?' said Grace. 'That would be fantastic. I'd love to show them our exhibit about Henry and Louise-Anne.'

Mr Grainger smiled at her. 'Indeed, I told them all about *The Thirteenth Body in the Mausoleum* and they would all love to see that particular exhibit, I can assure you. Anyway, I'll leave you all to it,' he said and went out again.

'You know,' Sarah said thoughtfully, 'we really should get a website for the museum, shouldn't we? If we put up photos and information, then all the Graingers could keep up with what we're doing – as well as everyone else, of course.'

Grace nodded. 'That's a great idea, Sarah,' she said. 'It would be good for visitor numbers, too. We'll talk to Josh and Daniel when we get to the house, seeing as they're the computer experts.'

Simone looked at her friends and smiled. 'Get a load of you lot,' she said. 'You really are dedicated to the museum, aren't you?'

'It kind of grows on you,' Sarah replied with a grin.

'I brought you something back from my trip,' Simone said suddenly. She got up and went over to the bookshelf and collected four small thick books. She handed one to each girl. 'Just a little something,' she said, blushing.

Sarah turned the brown leather-bound book over in her hands. It had a small silver lock attached to the front with a little silver key in it. She turned the key and opened it. 'A secret diary,' she said, delighted. 'Thanks so much, Simone.'

'I feel like Alice in Wonderland,' Hannah said, holding up the tiny key. 'I absolutely love it. Thank you.'

'You shouldn't have spent money on us,' Abi added, 'but it's an awesome gift.'

Simone shrugged. 'I just thought you'd like a diary, so you could keep notes about being ghost detectives – you know, like Beryl did.'

'That's a great idea,' Hannah said, her eyes shining at the thought. 'Just think, in a hundred years maybe some other girls will find these diaries, like we found Beryl's. It might continue the tradition.'

Sarah smiled at Hannah's enthusiasm – anything to do with writing or reading and Hannah practically swooned.

'I love the tiny lock,' Grace said, her bracelets

clinking as she turned her diary over in her hands. 'I'll write up everything that happened with the ghost of Louise-Anne.'

'And you can start writing in your next adventure, I presume?' Simone said, her eyebrows raised. She finally asked the question she'd been waiting to ask all along: 'So has the ghost gang been busy of late? Who has come looking for help while I've been away? Tell me everything.'

'No one, thankfully,' Sarah said heartily. 'Not a shimmer of a ghost since Louise-Anne left.' She had enjoyed cracking the mystery of Louise-Anne's past, but really, Sarah was just glad that she was the only ghost who had turned up. It had sort of unnerved her how quickly they had all started talking about ghosts as if they were perfectly normal. She would be glad to have the memory of Louise-Anne and leave it at that. She had no desire to be a full-time ghost detective, not by a long shot.

'Oh.' Simone looked disappointed. 'I thought you'd be busy dealing with a new ghost and solving another mystery.'

'I think it was a one-off crazy thing,' Sarah said dismissively. 'Maybe your granny was playing a trick on us. Who knows? But it's been almost a whole month now and we haven't had a whisper of any odd goings-on, so I think our ghost-detective days are behind us. And I, for one, don't mind in the slightest.' Sarah looked over at Abi, Hannah and Grace, but it was hard to tell if they agreed with her way of seeing things or not.

Simone regarded her four friends thoughtfully. 'Maybe those days are behind you,' she said finally. 'And maybe they aren't.'

2

Up and Running

'Well, *I* think that's a really stupid idea.'

Sarah bit her lip to stop the scream that was threatening to escape. She looked over at Abi and rolled her eyes. Abi nodded slightly, her face tight with annoyance. There was no doubt about it, Chrissy Edwards was quite simply a royal pain in the backside.

'If you ask *me*,' Chrissy went on in that full-of-herself voice of hers, 'we should do Twitter first, then do a website next year. Websites aren't really very cool, you know? You really haven't thought it through properly, Sarah.'

Sarah sighed deeply and counted to ten. All her thoughts of this being a good day disappeared. Obviously it was going to be a long day for the museum volunteers. But then wasn't it always when Chrissy was being like this?

Hiding behind Hannah's shoulder, Grace pulled a funny face at Sarah, to make her smile. Sarah thanked her lucky stars that she had such great friends to see her through moments like this. Left to her own devices, she'd probably have a shouting match with Chrissy and make everything worse, but her friends knew exactly when they needed to do something to distract her.

'Chrissy,' Sarah said as patiently as she could, 'do you not think a website is the easiest way to share all the information we want to give to people? It means we can put up photos and updates, all that kind of stuff, and it makes it look very official, too. That's why I'm suggesting it.'

'I think Sarah's right,' Josh said quietly. Abi smiled gratefully at him for backing up her friend. She blushed when he shot a smile back in her direction, then looked quickly at her friends to make sure they hadn't noticed. 'A website would be the best way to get more people interested in what we're doing,' he went on. 'There might even be other town museums that we could link to. It would definitely look more official than just tweeting about the museum.'

Chrissy flicked back her glossy black curls and glared first at Sarah, then at Josh. 'Well, I don't agree,' she insisted. 'Daniel,' she said, turning on her sweetest voice, 'you know all about this sort of thing, don't you feel that I have a good point?'

As ever when Chrissy tried to be charming to him, Daniel Binoche froze like a rabbit caught in headlights. Sarah watched with amusement as he shifted uncomfortably on his feet. It was obvious that Chrissy liked him and wanted to win him over, and just as obvious that he'd rather be smeared head to toe with honey and dropped into a bear pit. He cleared his throat. 'I think you're both on the right track actually because we need as much online presence as possible. But I'd say do the website first, then look at Twitter and the rest afterwards.'

Chrissy narrowed her eyes and looked very put out. Her friend Elaine jumped to take her side. Privately, Sarah and the girls called Chrissy's friends the Clones – they all tried to look, talk and act like her. Elaine was a prime example. Sarah could feel the anger rising in her again – she really hated when people didn't think for themselves and just tried to be 'cool'. It was crazy that Elaine couldn't see how silly it made her look to keep going along in Chrissy's shadow.

'Well, I'm voting for Twitter first,' Elaine announced, nodding her head at Chrissy.

'OK,' Sarah said, seeing her opportunity. 'Why don't we all cast a vote, then it's fair?' She knew Chrissy was fuming at this turn of events, but she couldn't shout down all of the eight other volunteers. 'Who thinks we should set up Twitter first?' Chrissy and Elaine's hands shot up in the air, but no one else joined them. 'Now who thinks we should try to get a website going first?' Sarah put her own hand up, followed quickly by Abi, Hannah, Grace, Daniel, Josh, Jack and Solomon.

Sarah forced herself not to smile – no point being petty about it. She just nodded briskly and said, 'Fine, we'll do a website and then set up other stuff after that. How will we go about it?'

'I don't mind working on the text for it,' Hannah offered quietly. 'If no one else wants to do it?'

The others shook their heads and Hannah looked delighted.

'And I could take photos of the place,' Jack added. 'Hannah, we can talk about what you want to write about, then make a list of shots I can do.'

Hannah smiled at him. 'Brilliant,' she said.

'Maybe you'd give me a hand, Grace,' Jack said, turning to her. 'You've a great eye for things, so you could sort of direct the photos.'

Grace grinned delightedly at him. 'Absolutely. And nice to see you've at last recognized my genius, Jack!' she teased.

Sarah noticed that Jack kept looking at Grace after she'd turned away. *Interesting*, Sarah thought.

'I've set up a small website before,' Josh said, 'so I'm happy to build it. Do you think you'd be able to give me a hand, Daniel?'

'Sure,' Daniel agreed.

Sarah looked around and smiled. 'Great, that's settled then. And, Chrissy,' she said, trying her best to be nice, 'why don't you look into the Twitter thing so we're ready to go on that afterwards?'

'Why don't you do it yourself, bossy-boots?'

Chrissy muttered angrily, then she stalked off towards the back stairs.

Sarah looked over at Elaine, who was standing there uncertainly, not sure how to make her exit. 'Elaine, I was genuinely trying to be nice,' Sarah said quietly. 'We all have to work together, so we may as well do our best to get on.'

Elaine blushed, but summoned her best sullen voice and said, 'Whatever,' then she followed her friend.

'Don't worry about them, Sarah,' Jack said cheerfully. 'And, by the way, that was some display there with Elaine. I don't think I've ever seen you being diplomatic before!'

Sarah punched his arm playfully. 'It was worth a shot,' she said, smiling at him, 'but I think normal services will now resume. There's just no point trying with some people.'

'Now that's the Sarah we know and love,' Jack said with a laugh.

There was the sound of striding footsteps and their teacher, Miss Flood, marched into the reception area. She was wearing old gardening clothes, carrying a sweeping brush and her cheeks were rosy red from the cold. 'Perfect day for working in the garden,' she said happily. She had discovered a passion for the Grainger gardens and the volunteers barely saw her these days. She was always outside, dreaming up more jobs to do. 'Is anything the matter?' she asked when she saw them all standing in a huddle.

'No, Miss,' Grace said. 'We were just talking about setting up a website for the museum and sharing out the jobs.'

Miss Flood shook her head and smiled. 'You lot really are the best volunteers a museum could hope for. If you need any help, just let me know. Otherwise I'll trust you to get on with it. Now, are we ready for today's visitors?' The volunteers looked at each other and nodded. 'Marvellous,' Miss Flood said, looking distracted, and Sarah could tell her mind was already wandering back to the garden. 'I'll just finish sweeping the path outside and let you lot get on with it.'

She left and Jack grinned. 'That really is becoming her catchphrase, isn't it? "Let *you lot* get on with it", meaning definitely not her.'

Grace laughed. 'I know, sometimes I think she trusts us too much!'

'Wow!' Solomon shouted, interrupting them. 'Come here and look at this.' He was sitting at the reception desk, checking the emails to the museum's account. 'You will not believe who's coming to visit next Saturday.'

They all gathered around the desk, pushing to get a look at the computer screen. He grinned wickedly at them, making Hannah laugh.

'Come on, Solomon, out with it,' she teased him.

'Who could be so special that it's filled you with such delight at the prospect of meeting them? Ooh, is it the guy who wrote the book about the Grainger family?'

Jack shook his head in despair. 'You actually think some writer guy would be *that* interesting? Only you, Hannah Greene! I bet it's a supermodel visiting the town who wants to see the incredible museum we've created. I'm bagging that guided tour – I said it first!'

Sarah groaned. 'Seriously, you think an airhead model would be an interesting visitor? No way – it has to be someone with a brain to get Sol excited, some famous history professor or –'

'If you'd all shut up for a half a second, I can tell you,' Sol said, pretending to be annoyed. 'It's way more exciting than a supermodel and it's way more exciting than a writer. It's . . . a group of ghosthunters.'

'A group of *what*?' Daniel said, looking astonished.

'Get out of here!' Abi said, shaking her head, but casting an anxious glance at her friends.

'You're making that up, Sol,' Grace said, elbowing in beside him. 'Let me see that email.' Her eyes skimmed the screen, then she looked up at the rest of the volunteers in surprise. 'He's telling the truth.'

Sarah could tell that Solomon was thoroughly enjoying breaking this little nugget to them and watching their shocked reactions. She looked over at Grace, Abi and Hannah and they all looked worried. She felt worried herself – what if these ghosthunters walked in the door and immediately knew there had been a spirit about? Would they be able to tell what the girls had been up to? What if some random ghost told them about the ritual and Louise-Anne? And what if, Sarah thought with a shiver, they decided to tell the other volunteers or Miss Flood about it? She looked over at her friends again – what would happen if everyone discovered their secret?

'It's an email from Mrs Gloria Welsh,' Solomon went on. 'Listen: "Dear Grainger House Museum, I am the president of the Association of Registered Ghosthunters (ARGH) and we are planning a trip to your recently opened museum on Saturday 1 December. We will be six ghosthunters in all and we hope you can accommodate us for a guided tour. We are, of course, interested in the house and gardens, but we are also hoping that we might encounter some supernatural phenomena during the course of our visit. We are all highly attuned to the spirit world and regularly make trips to old houses to see what we can find. There is nothing to be afraid of, however, as if we do make contact, it will be limited to ourselves and we won't invite the spirits to interact with anyone else. We are very much looking forward to it and plan to be there at three p.m."' Solomon looked up from the screen.

'What do you think of that?' he asked, relishing their surprised faces.

The volunteers looked at each other, unsure what to say – all except Jack, of course. 'Well, I can't wait to meet them,' he announced. 'What do you think a ghosthunter looks like? Will they be in black clothes and wearing strings of garlic?'

'Maybe they'll have those little machines – what are they called?' Daniel said, tapping his head with his finger.

'Geiger counters?' Josh suggested.

'Yeah,' Daniel said, 'those little devices that click and make noises when there's a ghost around.'

'And maybe even those special cameras that record things we can't see,' Josh said, getting caught up in the idea. The four boys began to talk loudly all at once, conjuring up images of superhero-type ghostbusters.

Sarah looked at her friends and raised her eyebrows questioningly. 'Seriously,' she whispered, 'the last thing we need is a bunch of ghosthunters poking around here. Do you think they know about Beryl and that's why they're coming? Do you think anything will happen?'

'No it won't,' Grace said, but she looked less sure than she sounded. 'We haven't seen anything in weeks. It's been all quiet.'

Hannah looked nervously at them. 'I know, but it's still a bit . . . strange, isn't it?' she whispered.

'I mean, what if they're really good and can tell there's been something going on here?'

'Let's not worry about it,' Abi said firmly. 'We can stay out of their way as much as possible. It'll be all right.'

The front door opened and a group of kids started to stream in to the reception area, all bundled up in their winter woollies. They were booked in for the ten-fifteen a.m. tour, and the volunteers got busy welcoming them.

As Sarah moved across to start taking coats, something caught her eye. She looked up at the wide marble staircase and, for just a moment, she thought she saw a column of air shimmering unnaturally. She stopped and stared. Glancing quickly at her friends, she saw that Abi, Hannah and Grace were focused on the new arrivals and hadn't noticed anything. She looked up at the staircase again, but it all looked normal – she must have imagined it after all this talk of ghosts. She shook her head. *It's nothing*, she told herself sternly. *Absolutely nothing.*

3

Ghosthunters

The following Saturday morning, Sarah's alarm clock started beeping loudly at half past eight. She yawned and rolled over to knock it off. She opened one eye: it was a dark, quiet morning. The air beyond the duvet was December-chilled, so she snuggled down deeper and shut her eyes tightly.

From the kitchen, she could hear the sounds of her mother pottering about. Her brother, Aaron, had football; practice around nine, then he was going to spend the day with their dad. She knew her dad wanted her to go along too, but she had told him the museum came first on Saturdays. She sighed to herself, thinking about how he had gone quiet on the phone when she'd said that. She didn't know if she'd really wanted to hurt him – maybe a little bit. Even though he had been gone since August, it still felt so unreal to have only three of them in the house. She felt she couldn't say it to anyone, but she really hated it.

Her mobile lit up and vibrated suddenly, saving

her from thinking about her dad any more. She reached over and grabbed it. It was a message from Grace:

Meet you girls in writing room @ 10.10.

The message had obviously gone to Abi and Hannah as well. Sarah wondered what Grace needed to talk about – probably something to do with the dreaded ghosthunters. Well, no point putting it off any longer – this day had to get underway some time.

When Sarah reached the museum, she could see immediately that the other volunteers were in high spirits, giddy at the prospect of seeing some ghosthunting in action. *If only they knew,* Sarah thought grimly. *Ghosts aren't exactly easygoing, if Louise-Anne was anything to go by. They could throw tantrums and generally make life unpleasant if they felt like it. We seriously don't want some ghosthunters unleashing a pile of spirits all around us – no matter how exciting they all think that sounds.*

The boys were gathered in the reception area and were trying to outdo each other with gruesome ghost stories, hoping to rattle one another. Chrissy and Elaine had elbowed in beside them, taking the opportunity to hang out with the boys and be part of the fun. Sarah suppressed a smile as she watched

Chrissy trying to stand ever closer to Daniel, and Daniel taking tiny shuffling steps away from her, trying just as hard to keep a bit of space between them. Sarah knew Chrissy wouldn't give up easily. Poor Daniel!

She looked for her friends, but couldn't see them, so she guessed they were already in the writing room. The others weren't paying her much attention, so she quietly walked over to the drawing room and went inside, with a final look over her shoulder to make sure she wasn't being observed. She closed the door with a gentle click, then raced to the hidden door that led to the writing room they had discovered on their second day at the museum. Sarah and her friends had only ever told Simone about this secret annex. No one else knew, and they wanted to keep it that way. Sarah couldn't explain it properly, but the room felt like a private space, a place that shouldn't be treated as just another room. She and the girls wanted to keep it for themselves. They certainly didn't want Chrissy or Elaine finding their way in there, that was for sure. She pushed the hidden mechanism and the secret door sprang open softly.

As she stepped inside, she saw Grace dusting the high window frame, using a long multicoloured feather duster. Her hair was tied up in a red cloth, and she was wearing bright yellow jeans with her volunteers' T-shirt.

'What are you doing, Mrs Mop?' Sarah asked, laughing.

Grace looked over and stuck out her tongue. 'I'll have you know I'm particularly fashion-forward this morning,' she said. 'And I felt this place needed a bit of TLC, so I brought my feather duster.'

'Of course you did,' Sarah teased her. 'Wait, don't tell me, is it Dolce and Gabbana or Chanel?'

Grace giggled and shook the duster at Sarah.

Abi and Hannah were standing at the old writing desk, and they both looked worried.

'Well, today's the day,' Abi said, biting her lip. 'The ghosthunters are coming. Jeez, I wish it was over already. I keep thinking up more things to worry about – like maybe they'll put a curse on the house or that the Geiger counter thing will go off the scale when they come near us.'

'Erm, it only does that for ghosts, Abi,' Sarah said pointedly. 'I'm pretty sure we're all flesh and blood here.'

Abi sighed impatiently. 'You know what I mean, Sarah,' she said. 'I'm just worried about the whole visit.'

Sarah wasn't looking forward to it herself, but she could see that Abi and Hannah needed to calm down.

'Come on, there's no need to get so worked up about it,' she said gently. 'They'll have a look around, find nothing and go off to find the next supposedly haunted house. They're not going to be expecting a bunch of kids to be . . . you know . . . ghost detectives. Besides,' she went on, 'we haven't detected anything remotely ghost-like since Louise-Anne left.' In her mind's eye she saw again the strange shimmer she thought she had seen on the staircase, but she dismissed it quickly.

Hannah nodded, but looked at Sarah thoughtfully. 'So why are we here?' Abi asked curiously.

Grace stood the duster against the wall and straightened up. 'OK,' she said, 'it's nothing bad. I just had an idea about the diaries Simone gave us.'

Hannah finally turned her gaze from Sarah and looked at Grace with great interest. 'I've already written about Louise-Anne and Henry in mine,' she said. 'What were you thinking about them?'

'Well, I just thought we could all keep our diaries in here,' Grace said. 'In the writing desk, like Beryl did. Then we can use this place to write up stuff and keep it all private.'

'I love that idea,' Hannah said with a smile. 'And I really love the idea of sitting in here writing. I'm all for it.'

'Sure,' Abi agreed. 'I've written all about our first ghost-detecting case. I'd hate anyone at home to find it and read it, so I'm happy to leave my diary in here.'

Grace turned to Sarah. 'What about you, Sarah? Did you write anything in yours?'

Sarah shifted on her feet, feeling a little uncomfortable. 'Yeah, I wrote a bit about it,' she admitted.

'Did you?' Grace sounded surprised.

Sarah shrugged. 'Well, Simone went to the trouble of buying it for me, so I thought I should actually use it.' She knew her friends expected her to be less into it than them, but once she had started writing she'd found she couldn't stop. It was like a weight off her shoulders to be able to put on the page the things she had thought and felt since her dad had left. 'I'm with Abi,' she continued, 'I don't want nosey Aaron to find it, so leaving it here makes sense.' She remembered some of what she'd written and asked anxiously, 'But we won't be actually reading each other's, will we?'

'No, I think we shouldn't,' Grace said. 'That's why I brought these.' From her pocket, she pulled out four satin ribbons. 'We can wear our keys round our necks,' she explained.

'Great idea,' Abi said, reaching out for the green ribbon. 'Anyone mind if I take this one?'

'I'll have purple,' Hannah said, and Grace handed it to her.

'Navy or red?' Grace said, holding up the last two ribbons in front of Sarah.

'I'll have the navy, I think,' Sarah said.

Grace beamed. 'Perfect – red's my favourite colour. Or at least, it is this month! Red is such a Christmassy colour.'

The four friends pocketed their ribbons and quietly made their way back outside.

That afternoon the volunteers gathered in the reception area, waiting for the ghosthunters.

'No way!' Jack argued. 'I mean, hunter has to mean man, doesn't? I reckon it's six big brave lads, for sure.'

'I don't know,' Daniel replied. 'Aren't women always said to be good at sensing stuff? I think it'll be a mix, and the women will have long hair and bangles, like Grace.'

'I don't care how they wear their hair,' Chrissy said, 'they are going to be crazy people. That much I can tell you right now.'

'They're here!' Jack called excitedly from his lookout post at the window.

A minibus pulled up slowly on the driveway in front of the house and its door hissed open. Jack turned from the window and hurried to the reception desk. 'Are we all ready?' he asked, his eyes wide in antipation.

'As we'll ever be,' Sarah whispered drily to her friends. The girls were standing apart from the others, watching from the door to the drawing room. They wanted to get a good look at these ghosthunters, and be able to scoot away quickly if they felt they were likely to start spouting anything about what had been going on in the house. The four girls looked at each other, then looked towards the front door. Sarah took a deep breath.

The door swung open and ten pairs of eyes stared as a white-haired lady stepped into the hall. She wore a tweed trouser suit with an ARGH badge on her lapel. She smiled brightly as she took in the reception and the volunteers.

'Good afternoon,' she said cheerfully. 'I'm Gloria Welsh. I emailed you last week. Is it OK to bring the others in for the tour?'

Sarah looked at her friends and grinned – if the rest were like granny Gloria, she reckoned they could breathe a sigh of relief. 'She looks totally harmless anyway,' she said out of the corner of her mouth.

'Not exactly what I had in mind,' Hannah said, trying not to laugh. 'And just look at Jack's face – he's so shocked.'

Jack was staring, open-mouthed, looking Gloria up and down, an expression of utter disappointment on his face. All his dreams of macho ghostbusters and a spooky showdown had been shattered by the appearance of Gloria. As she made her way outside to call her fellow ghosthunters, Jack slumped into a chair. 'Ghosthunters, my bum,' Sarah heard him mutter to himself, and she shook with quiet laughter.

The rest of them climbed down from the minibus and made their way inside. They were all women, all elderly, all neatly dressed and chattering together like excited birds. They looked like they were on an outing for tea and scones, not preparing to hunt down ghostly beings from the afterlife.

'If you want me to mind the Geiger counters, that's fine,' Sarah said to the four boys. Jack frowned at her and she burst out laughing. 'Or any of the rest of their hi-tech equipment, for that matter. Seriously, I'm here to help.' She shook with laughter again – probably more out of relief, she thought to herself, than anything else.

'Ha, ha,' Daniel said sarcastically. 'You're so witty, Sarah.'

'We didn't actually think they were going to be kick-ass ghostbusters,' Josh said defensively. 'We were only having fun with the idea.'

Abi looked at him in surprise. 'Oh now, don't you try to kid us otherwise, Josh Fitzsimons. You lot have been building up this encounter for the past week. You did too think it was going to be all night-vision goggles and deathly screams.'

Josh tried to frown at her too, but he could never stay annoyed with Abi. One look at her and he couldn't help smiling. His face broke into a smile now and he looked sheepish. 'OK, we thought it would be a little bit exciting. Looks like we were getting ahead of ourselves.'

They greeted the ladies, took their coats and umbrellas and Solomon and Daniel set off to give them the guided tour. As they headed towards the ballroom, Sarah heard one of the lad... you feel a chill in the air? Anyone? I've ... we might have some spirits nearby!'

Grace shook her head and smiled. 'I think the... going to be as disappointed as the boys are,' sh... whispered. Sarah sent up a silent wish that Grace would be proved right.

Solomon and Daniel toured the group around the house and gardens. Jack joined them a few times, just to see if anything ghostly was happening, but each time he returned to the other volunteers with a long face. 'Nothing,' he complained bitterly. 'They just keeping closing their eyes and "communing", whatever that means. I can tell you that it doesn't mean we get to see any actual ghosts, or vampires for that matter.'

Chrissy snorted. 'Vampires? You're as crazy as they are, Jack, if you actually thought those old nutters were going to call someone from beyond the grave! I'd say they'd have trouble calling someone on the phone!'

Elaine doubled over laughing at this. 'You're so funny, Chrissy,' she gasped. 'That's hilarious.'

'Oh, where's your sense of adventure, Chrissy?' Jack said crossly. 'This place is ancient, you'd think we could find *something* ghostly about here.'

Just then, Solomon and Daniel led the group down the wide marble staircase and back to the reception area. The women seemed delighted with their visit and gathered round the desk to ask questions and pick up copies of the museum brochure. Miss Flood arrived in from the garden and came to greet them.

'You have done a wonderful job here,' Gloria said, smiling widely. 'And these children are a credit to you and their school. They have treated us so well, and our lovely tour guides were so informative. It's really very impressive.'

Sarah could see that Miss Flood was delighted with the compliments. 'Thank you so much,' she replied. 'Yes, the ten volunteers are brilliant – very dedicated to the place, I have to say –'

'So did you find any ghosts?' Chrissy interrupted. 'I mean, that was the point of the visit, wasn't it?'

Gloria nodded. 'Yes, we very much hoped to encounter some spirits, but, alas, no. Apparently one of the original family members was a witch, perhaps even a ghosthunter, so we thought it would be a good spot. Not today, I'm afraid.'

'Have you *ever* seen a ghost?' Chrissy asked, and Sarah could hear the mocking tone in her voice. Why she would want to insult this group of nice ladies, Sarah couldn't understand. Plus, Chrissy was looking for trouble if she was rude to visitors in front of Miss Flood.

Gloria looked a bit annoyed by Chrissy's manner. 'Yes, I have young lady,' she answered sharply. 'I have seen many, many ghosts in my time. You shouldn't think yourself above such things, you know.'

'What was your favourite sighting?' Abi asked enthusiastically. Sarah knew she was trying to make up for Chrissy's rudeness. That was so like Abi, to try to make everyone feel better.

Gloria smiled at Abi and thought for a moment. 'Well,' she said at last, 'there was a particularly insistent spirit we met in Longfall Castle . . .'

As Gloria started to tell her story, Sarah suddenly became aware of a dull thudding sound overhead. She looked up to the ceiling, wondering what it could be. *Maybe someone's up there shifting some furniture*, she thought. She looked around the reception and realized that all of the volunteers were present, and Miss Flood. There was no one left to be upstairs. The thudding sound came again, rhythmic this time, like a foot beating time to music. Sarah looked up, puzzled.

'Is something wrong, Sarah?' Solomon asked her quietly.

'Can you hear noises upstairs, Sol?'

He cocked his head to one side and listened. 'Nope,' he said after a few moments, shaking his head. Then he looked sharply at her. 'Oh, I get it,' he said, 'you're trying to wind me up that there is a ghost about for them to bust. Well, forget it, Sarah, I'm not falling for that.' Sarah looked at him in surprise – Solomon was usually so polite, it wasn't like him to lose his temper with anyone.

There was a loud thud then, like someone

jumping up and down. 'Well you must have heard that,' Sarah said looking towards the ceiling.

Sol shook his head. 'Nice try, Sarah, but, like I said, try it on with someone else.'

'. . . then the ghost appeared before us,' Gloria was saying, 'and a deathly chill descended on the room . . .'

Sarah could hear the thudding sounds very clearly now. As Solomon walked off in disgust, she moved over beside Grace. She didn't have to say a word.

'You're hearing that?' Grace said immediately.

'Solomon couldn't,' Sarah said quietly. 'It's really loud.'

Grace nodded and glanced anxiously towards the ceiling. 'It's like . . . leaping or dancing or something.'

Hannah walked over to join them. 'Can you two hear weird sounds upstairs?' she whispered. 'It's freaking me out.'

'We hear it,' Sarah nodded, 'but it doesn't look like anyone else does.'

'. . . I felt fear gripping my heart then and I grabbed the hand of Margaret – didn't I, Margaret? I was rooted to the spot with terror. Oh, you children cannot begin to understand what it's like to see a sight like that.'

Abi was nodding at Gloria's story, her eyes wide with listening. The boys were hanging on her every word, too, delighted to be getting an exciting story at last. Sarah, Grace and Hannah were looking at Abi, trying to work out if she was hearing the thumps overhead when they suddenly saw their friend's face go white. She was staring above Gloria's head towards the staircase. Her smile had frozen on her face.

Very slowly, Sarah, Grace and Hannah all turned to look at the stairs. Sarah gasped – the column of air was shimmering, just like before. *Oh no, no, no,* she thought frantically, *not now. Not in a room full of ghosthunters.*

As the four girls watched, the shimmering started to fade and in its place appeared . . . a ghost, a child ghost. She was dressed in a ballet costume, with a black leotard, pale pink tutu, nude tights and white ballet shoes, with her hair scraped back into a tight bun. She stood on the stairs, staring fixedly at them.

Sarah felt like her brain had turned to jelly. The ghosthunters were standing between the staircase and the desk, just steps away from the ballerina ghost, but seemed totally oblivious to her presence. The girls could feel goosebumps standing up on their arms. Sarah looked at the members of the ARGH, but they weren't registering this ghost at all. She couldn't believe it! She looked from Abi to Hannah and Grace and she knew they were all seeing the little girl too, and were as paralysed as she was.

On the stairs, the ghost raised her hand and pointed up to the first floor, then the air shimmered once more and she vanished.

'. . . so that was our incredible spirit encounter,' Gloria finished with a flourish. 'What do you think of that?' she asked, looking around at her audience's rapt faces.

Sarah, Grace, Hannah and Abi were thinking only one thing: *What do we do now?*

4

The Dancer's Story, Sort of

Miss Flood waved off the ghosthunters' minibus and came back inside.

'Wonderful job, everyone,' she said, smiling at her volunteers. 'Was that the last tour for the day?'

'Yep, that's it,' Jack answered. 'Shall we start clearing up, Miss?'

'Of course, just go around and give each room the once-over and let's all get home for dinner.'

The volunteers started to drift off to check the various rooms. Sarah shook herself free of the spell the sight of the ghost had cast over her and walked quickly towards the stairs. 'I'll do the rooms on the next floor,' she announced loudly. 'Give us a hand, will you?' she called to her friends, nodding urgently at them. Abi, Hannah and Grace still looked a bit dazed, but they nodded back and made their way to the stairs.

Once at the top, the four friends looked uncertainly at each other.

'My goodness,' Abi said, her eyes wide, 'I can't

believe we've got another one. I nearly dropped to the floor when I looked up and saw her there.'

'They were some ghosthunters, weren't they?' Sarah said with a weak grin. 'I mean, she was right behind them – how did they not feel it? All that "communing" and they couldn't tell when a ghost was practically standing on their toes!'

They started giggling nervously, which quickly turned into near-hysterical guffawing as they stuffed their hands into their mouths, trying not to explode with laughter. Grace and Sarah were bent double, scarcely able to catch their breath. Even though they had been through this with the ghost of Louise-Anne, they were still rattled by the sudden sighting of the little girl ghost. Sarah couldn't tell if she was more annoyed, frightened or excited by the whole thing – everything was mixed up inside her.

'I really thought we were finished with this,' Hannah said, finally composing herself. 'Do you think we're going to be like Beryl and have ghosts turning up for the rest of our lives?'

The girls stopped laughing abruptly at that thought.

'I seriously hope not,' Sarah said, shaking her head. 'We're only twelve – that might mean something like seventy years of unhappy ghosts!'

'Jeez, way to make the future sound good, Sarah,' Abi groaned, making them dissolve into giggles again.

'Which room do you think she's in?' Grace whispered. As she spoke, the thudding sounds started up again and it was plain the noise was coming from the nursery down the hall. The girls stood there, looking at the door to the nursery. 'Anyone want to go first?' Grace asked nervously.

'Sarah?' Hannah asked.

'Me?' Sarah gasped. 'Why should I do it?'

Hannah was staring hard at her. 'I just have a funny feeling,' she began, narrowing her eyes, 'that maybe you knew something about this before now?'

Sarah couldn't believe it – Hannah was like a truth detector. Since they were five, Hannah always seemed to know whenever Sarah was lying. She thought back to the moment in the writing room when she had pictured the strange shimmer she hadn't told them about and she knew in her gut that Hannah had seen something on her face in that moment that had given her away.

'You're very quiet over there, Sarah,' Hannah said, prodding her. 'Nothing to say?'

Sarah opened her mouth to protest, but she knew she'd been rumbled. She also knew, from the look on Hannah's face, that her friend was a bit angry with her for holding out on them. 'All right,' she sighed, 'I suppose I deserve that. It wasn't on purpose, though, I promise. I wasn't sure what I'd seen on the stairs and after all this ghosthunter talk, I thought I had just imagined it.' She chanced a smile at her friends. 'Anyway, I'd rather face a ghost any day than the wrath of Hannah Greene.'

Hannah bit back a smile – she knew her friend so well.

Sarah threw back her shoulders and marched towards the nursery, the other girls following closely behind. She put her hand on the doorknob, took a deep breath and pushed open the door. There, in the middle of the room, was the little ballerina, turning a *plié* on the wooden floor. *Thump!*

For a ghost, she sure manages to make a lot of noise, Sarah thought to herself.

The girl came to a rest, standing perfectly poised, and watched them as they filed through the door. 'Finally!' she said in an impatient voice. 'I thought I'd have to go down there and drag you up.'

Sarah heard the door close behind them as Grace pushed it shut, and then they were alone with the ghost. Now that she could get a good look at her, Sarah could see that the girl was probably no more than ten years old. She looked skinny and a bit gawky in her tight ballet costume. She jutted out her chin defiantly as she examined them, but Sarah couldn't help thinking she seemed just like her own brother, Aaron – putting on a show of confidence, but inside very unsure of herself. Sarah decided that while the ghost girl was trying to look in control, her eyes betrayed the fact that she really felt lost and sad.

What could have happened to her? Sarah thought.

She decided to be direct. 'Hi, I'm Sarah,' she said, her voice high and unnatural. 'These are my friends, Abi, Hannah and Grace.' The girls smiled at the ghost encouragingly. 'Who are you?' Sarah asked.

'I'm Felicity Fenston,' the girl replied.

Silence. Sarah grappled for the right question – she had always managed to rub Louise-Anne up the wrong way and she didn't want to make that mistake again.

'Tell us how you died,' she said at last.

The ghost flinched. 'Why would you want to talk about that?' she demanded angrily.

Sarah glanced at her friends and her glance said: *Help!*

Abi stepped forward immediately.

'Erm . . . we just need to know about you, so that we can figure out how to help you,' Abi said gently.

'I know exactly how you can help me,' Felicity said firmly. 'You have to get me to Snow White.'

Abi's eyebrows shot up her forehead as she struggled to comprehend what the ghost was saying, and Sarah had to fight the urge to burst out laughing. She took a deep breath to control herself. She could see that Hannah and Grace were in the same boat. *Get me to Snow White* – was this girl for real? Sarah decided Abi's gentle approach might take a while to get through to the ghost, so she stepped in again herself.

'Well, technically you could say Snow White is dead,' Sarah began as gently as she could – this was a ten-year-old kid after all, 'so it won't be possible for us to call her up, you know, to appear before us,' she said, hoping Felicity would understand. If this didn't work, she'd have to break it to her gently that Snow White was just a made-up person in a story!

Felicity stared at her as if she'd just started talking gibberish.

'Please tell me you're not really stupid enough to think I came all the way here to meet a fairy-tale character?' Felicity crossed her arms and stared at Sarah with a mixture of defiance and triumph, clearly enjoying being rude and catching Sarah off guard.

Sarah's cheeks flushed red. 'Now listen here, you . . . you . . . dead dancer girl –' she huffed.

'Whoa! Time out!' Abi called out. 'Hang on, Sarah,' she hissed, 'don't talk to her like that.'

'That's harsh,' Grace whispered fiercely. 'She's just a kid.'

Sarah blushed with embarrassment and hung her head, feeling ashamed of her outburst. 'Sorry,' she mumbled.

The ghost seemed to be enjoying the scene. 'You should listen to your friends,' she said pointedly to

Sarah. 'I'm just a kid, remember.' She stuck out her tongue at Sarah, and it was all Sarah could do not to take the bait. She bit the inside of her mouth, hard, and didn't reply. Oh yes, this girl was just like her brother all right – just when you were feeling sorry for them, they went and said something like that and all you wanted to do was throttle them. Sarah looked over at Abi and nodded at her – she'd stay quiet from now on and let Abi do this bit.

Abi stepped forward and addressed Felicity again. 'OK, let's start over,' she said in a calm voice. 'You've come to ask our help, right? So how can we help you?'

'I need to get to *Snow White*,' Felicity repeated. 'It's the show my ballet school is putting on and I'm dancing in it tonight, at eight o'clock. It's really important that I get there on time. I'm Snow White, which means I'm the star.' *There's the jutting chin again*, Sarah thought. 'That's why I need your help.'

Abi was at a loss – didn't the girl realize that the show was long over? 'What age are you, Felicity?' she asked gently.

'I'm ten. What age are you?'

'Twelve,' Abi said. 'And when did you . . . pass over?'

'The twenty-second of December 2006,' Felicity said offhandedly, as if the whole notion of it bored her.

43

'And how . . .?' Abi began, then stopped. She could feel tears at the back of her eyes. This little ballerina was so young – Abi wasn't even sure she wanted to know how she had died. 'How . . . did it happen? Did you get sick, perhaps?'

Felicity set her mouth in a hard line. 'I don't know what you're talking about that for. I just need to be Snow White! You have to get me there. I'm going to be *late*.' She stamped her foot in exasperation and goosebumps skittered across Sarah's skin.

'And we really want to help you,' Abi said quickly. She looked around for inspiration. 'Hey, do you think this room has anything to do with why you're here?' she asked. 'Does it mean anything to you?'

Felicity looked around, as if seeing the room for the first time. 'This place? No. My mum used to bring me up here for fitness training in the grounds, but that's all.' She looked around at the beautifully decorated nursery. The volunteers had recreated it, based on a photograph in the book on the Grainger family that was downstairs in the library. It had pale yellow curtains held back with white sashes, and there was writing going right round the walls, up near the ceiling, with the words from 'Rock-a-bye Baby'. The wooden floor was polished and on a soft white rug stood a gorgeous rocking cradle with a white linen hood. There was a tall chest of drawers, a rocking chair, an ornate fireplace and shelves for books and toys. It was a rich woman's nursery for sure.

44

'It is lovely, though, isn't it?' Felicity said softly, seemingly transfixed by the little room. 'They must have loved this baby.' A look crossed her face, but Sarah couldn't say what it was. As soon as it appeared, it was gone, and Felicity's expression hardened again. 'So how are you going to help me?'

The girls looked at one another, lost for words yet again.

'We'll try to find out about the performance,' Abi said. 'Then we'll see what we can do to help. What was the name of your ballet school?'

'Was it the bolshy ballet?' Sarah muttered under her breath. Abi shot her a warning glance.

'The Roseman Academy,' Felicity replied.

'I know that place,' Hannah said. 'It's not far away. My cousin used to go there.'

'OK,' Abi said, 'then we'll Google it and find out what we can.' She frowned. 'Oh right – you probably don't know what that is. Google is part of the Internet, which is –'

Felicity stamped her foot again and pouted. 'Thanks for the lecture, but I *know* what the Internet is. When I said 2006, I didn't mean BC.' With that the air shimmered and she disappeared.

The girls were silent for a minute, staring in astonishment at the place where she'd been standing.

'Seriously, I prefer working with old ghosts,' Sarah said quietly. 'Preferably last century.'

Grace smiled. 'It's all an act,' she said, shaking

her head in wonder at this new arrival, who was so different from their previous encounter. 'You can just see that she's really a scared little girl, but she's trying so hard to hide it.'

Sarah nodded and sighed. 'Yeah, I know,' she agreed. 'She did annoy me, but it was in the same way Aaron annoys me. All the while, I know he's really saying something else, if you know what I mean.'

'Listen, I know about little brothers – I have three of them, remember?' Grace said with a grin. 'I know *exactly* what you mean.'

'So what are we going to do next?' Abi asked, looking around at them. 'This is going to be difficult. I don't really see how we can help her.'

'I think,' Hannah said thoughtfully, 'that she maybe doesn't realize that she's dead. The way she kept going on about the performance and she absolutely refused to tell us anything about how she died. Maybe she can't talk about it because she hasn't accepted it's real.'

Sarah looked at Hannah in admiration – she had such a sensible head on her shoulders. She would never have roared at Felicity like Sarah had. Sarah felt another stab of shame. Why couldn't she be more like her friends and stay calm and reasonable?

'That's a really good way of looking at it, Hannah,' Grace said. 'How about we check Beryl's diary, see if she said anything about ghosts who don't know they're, you know, ghosts? Simone said we could have a look at it whenever we needed to.'

'Good idea,' Hannah said, nodding her head. 'That's as good a place as any to start. Then we can search for Felicity on the Internet and see if we can find out any of her secrets.'

5

Surfing for Clues

The following day was Sunday, and Hannah sent around a text suggesting they all come over to her house. She could ask her mother for permission to use her laptop, and they could attempt to unravel Felicity's story.

When Sarah got the text, she muttered to herself and fired off an answer.

'My word,' her piano tutor said, looking at her over the top of the sheet music she was reading, 'I hope you play that quickly and confidently when we start.'

Sarah smiled apologetically. 'Sorry, I just had to send one message.' She was dropping her phone into her bag when Hannah's reply flashed up:

No prob. How about the Internet cafe near music school instead ? Meet there after lesson. One hour?

Sarah smiled. *Yes!* She had time to do a quick smiley-face reply and then she had to put away the phone and give her mind over to the music of Chopin.

She practised for over an hour before Miss Cooper released her. Sarah threw her stuff into her bag and raced out the door. The girls would already be there by now, but it was only a five-minute walk – which meant a two-minute run.

At the cafe, her friends were waiting for her. They had bought four glasses of juice and paid to use a computer for thirty minutes. Hannah chose a corner seat by the window and Abi and Grace followed her over.

'We can sit here and watch Sarah come hurtling down the street,' Hannah said with a mischievous smile. 'I guarantee she'll be a blur of red hair, running like a maniac. She's always late!'

Abi and Grace laughed and pulled up some extra chairs.

'Did you see who's over the far side?' Abi asked, looking towards the opposite corner window seat. 'Daniel,' she said, pointing across.

'Hi, Daniel,' Grace called out loudly and gave him a little wave.

He looked a bit startled to see them, but he smiled and waved back. 'Hey, Grace,' he called over. 'I'm just finishing up here.'

He started gathering his things and then walked over to their table. 'I thought I was the only geek who came to a place like this on Sunday,' he said, grinning at them. 'What are you up to?'

Grace looked flustered for a moment. 'Abi thought she'd like to join a ballet class and we're just researching them.'

'Oh right,' he replied vaguely, as if the very word 'ballet' had made him lose interest. 'What about Sarah?' he asked looking around. 'Is she not with you?'

'She's on her way,' Grace explained. 'She's got extra piano tutorials at the moment because she's sitting a grade exam soon. But don't ask me which one – I can never remember how it works.'

Daniel looked very interested now. 'Sarah plays piano?' he said, sounding impressed. 'I didn't know that.' He glanced at his watch, as if deciding whether to stay or go. 'I'm getting a lift home with my mum,' he said. 'I'd better go. But . . . there was something I wanted to tell you.' He looked a bit unsure of himself. 'It might be nothing, but it's just . . . well, yesterday I overheard Chrissy talking to Miss Flood, and she was complaining about you four.'

'Complaining?' Grace said, surprised. 'What did we do?'

'According to Chrissy, you were rude to some customers and they left without doing the tour. She said it was mainly Abi and Sarah.'

Abi gasped. 'But that never happened,' she said,

50

shocked that Chrissy would make up pure lies about her.

'I didn't think it had happened,' Daniel said quietly, 'but she's obviously got a problem with you, so I'm just letting you know. She was saying that Tiffany and Sophie would love to be volunteers, so my guess is she wants to get some or all of you out.' He looked at his feet, then back up at the three friends, who were still struck dumb by Chrissy's meanness. 'Hey, sorry to be the one to tell you.'

'No, that's all right, Daniel,' Hannah replied. 'It's better to know so we can look out for her in future. She's been on the warpath ever since Abi and Josh tricked her the night of the launch.'

'I guess so,' Daniel agreed. 'Well, I have to get going. See you at school tomorrow.'

He headed towards the door. Abi looked at Grace and Hannah and shook her head. 'Can you believe that?' she demanded. 'She's some piece of work. I mean, how could she?'

Grace and Hannah looked equally angry. Chrissy could be a dangerous enemy, obviously. Hannah opened her mouth to speak, but suddenly her face broke into a smile. She nudged her friends and pointed outside. 'Look, here comes Sarah now,' she said. 'She'll be mad she missed him.'

Sarah pelted down the road, her scarf streaming behind her, and took a sharp turn left to skid through the cafe door. As she did so, she crashed straight into Daniel, almost knocking him over. Her green eyes registered surprise, then utter disbelief.

'Oh no, Daniel, I'm so sorry,' she said, blushing fiercely as he grabbed her arm to steady himself.

'I thought you said she was going to miss him,' Abi whispered. 'I'd say she just scored a bullseye!' The three girls giggled.

Hannah was watching Sarah and Daniel closely. 'Look at how he's looking at her!' she hissed.

Daniel was telling Sarah it was no problem, that he was OK – but he still had a hold of her arm. Grace winked at Abi and Hannah. 'Looks like he doesn't want to let her go, doesn't it?'

Finally, Daniel stepped round Sarah and with a final goodbye from him and a final blush from her they parted. Sarah seemed lost in thought for a few seconds as she watched him walk away, then she turned round to look for her friends – only to find them all staring at her, with odd smiles on their faces.

'What?' she said defensively. 'I didn't see him. It was an accident.'

'A very happy accident,' Grace said with a grin.

Sarah made a face at her and stomped over to the table, dropping her bag to the floor. She unwound her scarf, unbuttoned her coat and flopped into the empty chair. 'I think I just ran the two-minute mile,' she said dramatically, taking in deep breaths.

'Well, I think you're changing the subject,' Abi replied, wagging her finger at Sarah. 'So what about cute-boy Daniel? It looked like he likes you.'

'No he doesn't,' Sarah said, folding her arms across her chest. 'Don't go all American on me now, Abi Worthy. Seriously, Daniel is not remotely interested in me.'

'Oh now, don't be so sure,' Hannah chipped in, enjoying this little chance to tease Sarah as much as Abi and Grace were.

'Come on, Sarah,' Abi said, poking her playfully in the ribs, 'tell us your deepest, darkest thoughts on the gorgeous Daniel.'

'I really don't think *you*, of all people, should be trying to tease *me* about boys,' Sarah said pointedly.

Abi's brown eyes widened. 'What does that mean?' she asked.

'I have two words for you,' Sarah replied. 'Josh. Fitzsimons.'

'Ouch,' Grace screeched. 'Sarah gets a direct hit. It's in your court again, Abi.'

'W-what . . . I mean . . . what about him?' Abi stammered.

Sarah cupped her hand to her ear. 'Oh, what's that sound?' she deadpanned. 'I think it's the sound of tables turning, don't you?'

Grace and Hannah were in fits of laughter now, watching the two girls try to play innocent with each other.

'You're just changing the subject again, Sarah,' Abi said, frowning. 'Josh is just one of the guys.'

'Or perhaps, he's one hell of a guy, Abi dearest?'

Abi couldn't help it, she started laughing too. 'Don't be such a dork,' she replied. 'He's just Josh.'

Sarah cocked her head to one side and studied her friend. 'I think to me, Hannah and Grace he's just Josh, but I don't believe you for a minute. I've seen the way you smile at each other. There's something there all right.'

Abi opened her mouth to say something, but Sarah held up her hand. 'No, don't say another word. Let's just spare each other's blushes and leave it at that?'

'Sounds good to me,' Abi agreed. 'But Daniel does like you, you know.'

'Can I remind you that Chrissy Edwards has her eye on him?' Sarah said.

'So?' Abi shrugged. 'She's annoying and silly. He'd never go for her. You can't honestly think he'd prefer her over you?'

'I thought we were saying no more about it?' Sarah said, sounding more subdued now.

'All right, you two lovebirds,' Hannah cut in, 'we've got work to do, remember? The mystery of Felicity isn't going to solve itself. I think you'll have to call a truce for now.'

'Truce,' Sarah and Abi said at the same time, then grinned at each other.

Hannah swivelled round in her chair to face the computer screen. 'I'll check the ballet school first,' she said, tapping at the keyboard. The girls gathered in close, eager to see what they would find out about the late ballerina.

'OK, here's the website,' Hannah said, clicking on it. 'Right. Here we go. It says the Roseman Academy was founded twenty-four years ago by Marcella Roseman. Has taught hundreds of children . . . blah blah blah . . . looking for funding for a more suitable venue . . . Nothing much here anyway,' she said, shaking her head.

'Is there a past pupils list?' Grace asked.

'Doesn't look like it,' Hannah replied, scanning the contents. 'Oh, there's a photo gallery. I don't know if they'd have photos from 2006, though.' She clicked on the gallery and the page filled with images. Hannah scrolled down through them. 'Oh look, they do!' she exclaimed. One of the images showed a group of about twenty girls, all around Felicity's age. Under the image it said: The troupe preparing to perform *Snow White*, December 2006. 'She has to be in there,' Hannah said, leaning closer to examine the faces. 'Yes, that's her, at the front.'

In the front line, right in the centre, stood Felicity. She was wearing a big smile, but somehow it didn't seem to reach her eyes.

'Wait a second!' Sarah gasped. She leant out of her chair, practically pressing her nose to the screen.

'Does that girl in the third row look familiar to you?'

They all peered closely, then looked at one another in astonishment.

'It's Simone,' Grace said in disbelief. 'She did *ballet*?'

'Simone and ballet?' Hannah said in wonder. 'Who would have thought?'

'There's a list of the names there,' Grace said, pointing at the screen. 'Is it definitely her?'

Hannah checked the list. 'Yeah, we're right,' she said, still unable to believe it. 'And, look, the girl beside her is called Mia Roseman – she must be related to the owner.'

Sarah was delighted. 'I am going to have so much fun teasing Simone about this,' she said, smiling at the thought of it. 'Print it out, Hannah, and we can surprise her with it when she least expects it!'

'Hang on,' Hannah said excitedly, 'this means Simone actually knew Felicity. She'll be able to help us with all this. When we go over to look at the diary, we can ask her to tell us all about Felicity – and what happened to her and what she was like.'

Hannah scanned through the rest of the website, but there was nothing more of interest. It didn't mention anything about a pupil dying, which seemed a bit strange.

'I'll look up Felicity now,' Hannah said, typing in her name. The first link was to the local newspaper, the *Clarion*. It was an obituary notice. Hannah glanced at her friends anxiously, then clicked on it.

At the top of the page was a close-up photo of Felicity. She was staring directly into the camera and smiling.

Hannah read the article out loud:

The entire community was stunned at the news of the death of Felicity Fenston, daughter of Dr and Mrs Michael Fenston. Felicity was well known for her beautiful dancing – she was one of the star pupils of the respected Roseman Academy. On Thursday night last, the 22nd, Felicity should have been performing in the lead role of Snow White at the academy's Christmas performance. For reasons unknown, the young girl left her home around 6 p.m, alone. It is thought she was taking a circuitous route to the academy – perhaps to calm her nerves before the performance. She was walking along the narrow, badly lit road that skirts the west side of the Grainger estate when she was struck by a passing car. She never regained consciousness and died of her injuries the following day. Our thoughts are with her family, who have been left devastated by this terrible accident and their tragic loss. May she rest in peace.

There was silence as the four girls took in Felicity's sad story.

'Poor little Felicity,' Abi murmured, her voice soft with emotion. 'What a horrible thing to happen.'

'*May she rest in peace*,' Hannah repeated. 'The question is – why can't she?'

'I think we're back to your idea,' Grace said quietly. 'That she doesn't know she's dead, so she's trying to end her day as she planned to and dance in the big show. It's the only answer from what I can see here.'

'I agree,' Sarah said. 'We need to talk to Simone now – find out whatever she can tell us about the whole thing. And we need to find out if Beryl gave any instructions about ghosts who think they're still alive.'

Grace shook her head. 'I really don't like this. I do not want to tell a little girl that she's . . . does that mean she thinks she's going to see her mum and dad again? She'll be so upset . . .'

The four girls looked at one another. Why, oh why had they done the ghost-detective ritual in the first place? Right now, it seemed like the worst job in the world.

6

Telling the Truth

The girls didn't get a chance to visit Simone until the following Friday after school. Sarah texted her to let her know they needed to see her, and she texted back inviting them to drop by any time after four o'clock. They were eager to talk to her and find out more about their new ghost.

At ten past four the girls locked their bikes against the black railings by the lodge and made their way to the door of the funeral parlour. The door was ajar, so Grace pushed it open gently and popped her head in.

'Hi, Grace,' Simone called. She was standing at the reception desk with a box of make-up spread out in front of her and she was arranging all the blushers, foundations and lipsticks.

'Hey, Simone,' Grace called back. 'Ooh, make-up, can I have a look?' She bounded over to the desk as her three friends came in the door behind her. She glanced over the products, then snatched up a peachy-coloured blusher. 'That is a gorgeous

59

colour,' she said, turning it over in her hands. 'I can't wait until my mum lets me wear this stuff. Where did you get this? I'd love to buy it.'

Simone was looking at her with a half-smile, one eyebrow raised. Before she could answer, Grace had pounced on a brown eyeshadow. 'Now this I have to have,' she said breathlessly. 'This would really go well with my eyes, don't you think?' She twisted the cap and dabbed some of it on the back of her hand, then held her hand up to her eyes. 'Look, don't you think so?' she said, opening her eyes wide at Simone.

'Grace,' Simone said quietly, 'that's mortuary make-up.'

Grace dropped the eyeshadow as if it had burned her. Simone struggled to hold back a laugh.

But Sarah exploded with laughter. 'Seriously? Did you just try on a dead person's make-up? Yuck!' Poor Grace just continued to stand there, looking horrified.

'Oh, Grace,' Abi said, starting to laugh too. 'You weren't to know.'

'We'll have to start calling you Morticia,' Hannah joked.

'All right, all right, that's enough,' Simone said, smiling. 'Grace needs to get over that shock. Come on, let me put this away and we'll go and sit down.' She gathered up the rest of the boxes and tubes, closed the box and put it under the counter. Still giggling, the girls followed her down the hall and into the sitting room, where they all tumbled into armchairs and on to the couch.

'Are you OK, Grace?' Simone asked.

Grace nodded. 'It's just a weird idea, you know, to have dead people's stuff on your skin.' She grinned like her old self. 'I'm over it, don't worry.'

'So what did you need to see me about today?' Simone asked, curious as ever about what the girls were up to – she knew it wouldn't be a boring run-of-the-mill question, not with this lot.

'What can you tell us about Felicity Fenston?' Abi asked.

Simone started as if she'd been jolted by electricity. Her face went pale. 'Pardon?' she said, her voice wispy. 'Who?'

Abi glanced nervously at her friends. 'Felicity Fenston,' she repeated. 'We need to find out about her.'

Simone stared at Abi without speaking. Sarah couldn't believe the change that had come over her. What was it about Felicity that had shocked her? *Oh no*, Sarah thought suddenly, *perhaps they were really good friends and we've just brought all the sadness back to her.*

Before she could say anything, Abi was already speaking and sounding very upset. 'Oh, Simone, I'm so sorry. I never stopped to think of how it might affect you to hear her name. I should have . . . I'm sorry, I really am.'

Simone seemed to gather herself then. 'No, it's all right, Abi,' she said in a quiet voice. 'That was a big tragedy in the town. You just took me by surprise talking about it all of a sudden.' She swallowed and seemed almost afraid to ask her next question. 'Is she . . . is she here?'

Abi bit her lip, afraid of saying anything that would upset Simone again.

Sarah could see that her friend was shook up, so she answered for her. 'Yes, she is,' she said simply. 'She arrived last Saturday, in the nursery upstairs. We don't know how to help her and hoped you'd be able to give us some idea of her life.' Simone nodded slowly, still trying to take it all in. 'How well did you know her?' Sarah asked gently.

'I didn't really know her at all,' Simone replied.

'Really?' Sarah said, surprised. 'But you did the show together?'

'How do you know that?' Simone said sharply. 'I've never told you about doing ballet or anything.'

Sarah was shocked by Simone's angry tone. 'We saw you – on the website,' she explained quickly. 'We were looking up Felicity, and there was a photo of the cast of *Snow White*, and we recognized you. That's all.' Simone was acting so strangely – she couldn't understand it.

'Simone,' Abi stepped in again, 'I'm really sorry that this is hard for you. I'm sure everyone was upset about Felicity's death, but she's turned up and all she will tell us is that she has to get to the performance – she won't talk about anything else. We don't know what to do. That's why we're here. We never wanted to upset you, but we were hoping you'd be able to tell us about her and also . . . well, we'd like to look at the diary again, if we can, to see if Beryl mentioned anything about ghosts who don't know they're dead.'

'You think she doesn't know she's dead?' Simone asked, looking surprised.

'That's our theory,' Hannah said. 'We tried to ask how she passed over, but she refused to talk about it, and she's only talking about the last thing she planned to do, so, yeah, we think maybe she doesn't fully understand what's happened to her.'

Simone considered this for a moment. 'And that's all she said?' she asked. 'That's all she told you?'

Hannah nodded. 'That's all we have to go on.'

Simone took a deep breath and seemed calmer again. 'She was in my dance class,' she admitted, 'but we weren't friends. Felicity was very focused on her dancing, nothing else really mattered to her.' Simone smoothed down her black dress over her spider-web tights. 'Her mother was a pretty tough woman, she pushed Felicity constantly to be better, to try harder, to rehearse more – it was a bit insane. I used to feel sorry for her, having a mother like that.'

'Pushy stage mom?' Abi said. 'You see a lot of

63

that in kids' clubs in America. I used to feel sorry for those girls too. Their mothers worked them to the bone.'

'Exactly,' Simone said, nodding. 'That's what Felicity's mother was like, and nothing she did was ever praised. Whenever she practised or performed, her mother would sit with a notepad and pen, taking note of all her mistakes. She'd shout and embarrass her in front of everyone if she felt there had been too many.'

Sarah thought about the sweet face of the little girl in the obituary and her heart broke for Felicity. She must have felt so alone.

'Anyway,' Simone said, 'the night she died Felicity was due to play Snow White. She should have been back to the academy by six thirty, but she never turned up. We couldn't believe it because it was an important night – some scout from London was supposed to be there, and it was Felicity's big chance. Her mother was like a crazy woman in the week before the show. She even made her miss school so she could stay home and practise. It was during the interval we got word about what had happened to her. We didn't finish the show.'

Sarah was watching Simone carefully as she spoke, but it was impossible to know what she was thinking.

'What happened afterwards?' Grace asked. 'Does her family still live nearby?'

'No, they left town pretty quickly and moved to another place. I never saw her mum afterwards, but I heard she was really devastated by it. She said she couldn't live in the same house any more.'

'And what was Felicity doing out on that road?' Sarah asked.

Simone shrugged. 'No one knows,' she replied.

'The newspaper said she might have been walking to calm her nerves,' Hannah said. 'Do you think that could have been true?'

Simone's expression was guarded. 'I really have no idea.'

Sarah looked at her friends. 'The only way we're going to find out is from Felicity herself, I suppose.' They didn't look very convinced that it would be possible to get Felicity to talk about it.

'What does she look like?' Simone asked softly.

Sarah smiled. 'She arrived in full ballet costume, hair pulled back tight and we first heard her because she was turning *pliés* in the nursery overhead.'

Simone smiled a little. 'That sounds like her all right. I can't believe she's even practising in the afterlife.' She shook her head. 'So you want to check the diary?'

'Yes, if that's OK,' Sarah replied. 'Just in case Beryl can help us out.'

Simone nodded. 'No problem. I'll go get it.'

'Can we come with you down to the vault?' Grace asked eagerly. 'I'd love to see it again.'

'It's not in the vault,' Simone said, smiling at her. 'It's in my room.'

Grace's eyebrows shot up. 'Were you, by any chance, doing the ritual so you could join us on the dark side?'

Simone laughed. 'No, I told you, Beryl said it was a blessing and a curse, so I don't want to be a ghost detective. I was just reading it, trying to remember as much as I could about her.' She pulled herself out of the armchair and headed off to get the diary. The girls looked at one another, but they didn't dare say anything in case anyone overheard them. Sarah knew each of them was thinking the same thing as her: *What's up with Simone?*

The door clicked open again and Simone came back in with the diary in her hand and sat down. She began flicking through the pages. 'There was definitely something about ghosts not knowing they were ghosts,' she said. 'Just give me a second and I'll find it.'

Sarah stared into the fire and thought about Felicity. She'd have to be nicer to her next time. Even when the ghost was being annoying, she'd have to remind herself that it was all a front and she was just a little kid really. She should do the same for Aaron as well. He was so hurt and confused about their parents' separation that sometimes he lashed out at her. If he caught her in a bad mood, she lashed right back. Now, she realized that wasn't helping anyone. She made herself a promise that she'd change her ways.

'I have it,' Simone said. 'Yeah, she talks about it here.' She began to read Beryl's diary:

This last encounter was a trifle strange. I was working in the garden, pruning the rose bushes, when the air blurred around me. I waited to see who would appear, and suddenly saw a young man standing on the path, watching me. He looked to be in his early twenties, a very dashing young thing, but poorly dressed in a working man's clothes. He held a cloth cap in one hand and studied my work with great interest. I greeted him and asked how I could help. He looked surprised at that. 'I'm here to help you, ma'am,' he replied politely. 'I'm the new gardener. Old Tom hired me but last week.' This answer I had not expected and I was quite at a loss as to how to continue our exchange. Normally, my spirit visitors immediately divulge the reason for their presence, so why was this chap different?

I probed gently, asking him his name and how he had come to be here. 'Like I said, ma'am, Old Tom took me on,' he replied. 'I'm afraid I'm not acquainted with Old Tom,' I said. 'Where does he work?' The man regarded me with uncertainty now, which I took to mean my answers made no sense to him. 'Why, he be the head gardener of this place, Beaulieu Hall.' I knew where that was – it was a large house and estate about twenty miles away. 'Forgive me, I forgot momentarily,' I replied, my brain working feverishly to figure out why this ghost had sought me out.

By degrees, I came to understand that he did not know that he was dead. It sounds impossible, but obviously the shock of his premature departure from this life had affected him deeply, and he did not now understand the nature of his predicament. I asked leading questions, but to no avail – there was no sign of the light of truth breaking upon the darkness of his ignorance. I told him I was able to help those who had gone on to the other place, but he simply nodded politely and looked alarmed.

Eventually, he left me alone and I pondered the problem a long time. I went to the public records archives and searched for a man fitting his description and employed at Beaulieu Hall. After an intense search, I found him! There was a notice describing his death, which had occurred as a result of some unspecified illness, just one week after he began work in the gardens, hired by one Tom Levins. I had the pieces of the puzzle now.

I sat in the garden and waited. When he next appeared, I immediately told him – gently, but firmly – that we had an important matter to discuss. Very calmly but in detail, I described what I found out about his life and his death. I told him the plain truth, unembellished. I offered to show him the notice, if he so wished. I even offered to find out the whereabouts of his final resting place, should he wish to view it. In the end, that wasn't necessary. As I spoke, his *features assumed a look of deep sorrow and I saw recognition flash across his face. He didn't need to tell me – I knew he understood. He was silent for a time after I'd finished my speech, then he thanked me for my honesty, raised his hand in a final farewell and left, never to be seen again.*

I think I was lucky this time – I expected an emotional storm to break over my head, fuelled by his horror at his situation and his sorrow at being rent from the living. It didn't happen, but if I encounter such a misguided spirit again, I will certainly tread carefully.

Simone looked up from the diary and regarded the four girls, who were listening intently to Beryl's words. 'Tread carefully,' she repeated, looking at them pointedly.

'That makes sense,' Hannah said softly. 'I suppose all we can do is tell Felicity the truth and hope that it all clicks into place for her. But I can understand Beryl's warning too. It might not be easy.'

'I'll say,' Sarah said. 'If we tell her she's actually dead and won't see the people she loves any more, it'll tear her apart.' She groaned, picturing the scene in her mind's eye and flinching away from it. 'I really don't want to do this,' she whispered, putting her face in her hands.

'I don't think anyone does,' Abi agreed. 'But we don't have a choice, do we?'

'I'll print out the obituary tonight,' Hannah said, 'then we'll have that with us in case we need it.'

'You mean, we'll do it tomorrow?' Sarah asked, hoping against hope they could put it off.

'Yes,' Hannah said firmly. 'She has been in the dark about all this long enough. Tomorrow, we'll give her the truth and face whatever happens then.'

7

Breakfast

Sarah trudged down the stairs and made straight for the kitchen. She needed a good hot breakfast before she'd be ready to climb on to her bike and cycle out to the museum. In the kitchen, her mum was sitting at the table, reading a book.

'Morning, sweetheart,' she said softly when she saw her sleepy-headed daughter walk in.

'I know it is. Already!' Sarah exclaimed. 'I wish the nights were longer.'

Her mother laughed. 'You're not alone there,' she said, closing her book. 'Come on, sit yourself here and I'll make you a bowl of porridge.'

She made the porridge and a fresh coffee for herself and sat down beside Sarah. She watched her daughter as she absent-mindedly tucked her long hair behind her ear and began to blow on her porridge to cool it.

'Sarah,' her mother began, 'it's just a few weeks to Christmas now.'

Sarah looked up, wondering where her mother

was going with this. Her voice sounded nervous, which made Sarah nervous too.

Her mum fiddled with the handle of her cup. 'I was just thinking, you know . . . this will be our first Christmas when your dad's not here.' She looked up quickly to catch Sarah's reaction. Sarah felt her stomach flip over at the mere mention of her dad. She had been desperately trying not to think about Christmas for that very reason. She couldn't think of anything to say.

'It's just that we've been talking,' her mum went on, 'and what we hope to do is to have a family Christmas dinner here, all four of us. He would come over about midday and stay until about four, if that's OK with you and Aaron?'

Sarah shrugged. 'Sure,' was all she could manage.

Her mum bit her lip. 'Are you really sure, Sarah?' she asked anxiously. 'We can organize this any way you want. All your father and I want is to give you a good Christmas, regardless of our . . . problems.'

Sarah sighed and put down her spoon – there was no way she could eat now. She mostly tried to avoid talking about anything upsetting with her parents. Now her mother was giving her no option but to face up to it. She felt like she was being dragged underwater and couldn't breathe. She just wanted to run out of the room and not talk about it.

'It's OK, Mum,' she said quietly. 'Whatever you feel is best.'

Her mum reached over and put her hand over Sarah's. 'Nothing is best, Sarah, I know that. I'm so sorry for all this mess. I hate to see you and Aaron trying to deal with it.'

Sarah nodded, but felt tears pricking behind her eyes.

'Love, is there anything at all you want to ask me or talk about?' her mother asked. 'We've not yet had a proper talk about this.'

There were a million questions Sarah wanted to ask, but they bashed and blurred together in her head and she couldn't think where to begin. She wanted to say something wise and wonderful to make her mum feel better, but she just felt so lost and unsure about everything. Really, the world had looked like a scarier place ever since her dad had gone – his leaving had made it feel like anything was possible, and that wasn't a nice feeling.

She looked at mother and took a deep breath. 'Mum,' she finally said in a near-whisper, 'why did he go?'

'Well,' her mother said, twisting her watch strap fiercely, 'he . . . we didn't feel the same way any more. We weren't getting on terribly well – I'm sure you were aware of that. And in the end we felt it might do more harm than good, to everyone, if we kept living in the one house. There was no right decision, Sarah, we just made the best decision we could in the circumstances.'

Sarah nodded slowly. 'But was there a particular, like, incident or reason?' she persisted. 'Something that pushed him over the edge?'

'No, no, nothing like that,' her mother assured her. 'It was a long drawn-out thing, it was months and months of difficulties piling up on top of us. Why? Did you think it was something in particular?' she asked worriedly.

Sarah looked away. Half of her wanted to tell her mother everything – how she believed in her heart that it was all her fault that her parents had split up – but the other half just refused to say it out loud. Instead, she nodded again and attempted a small smile. 'Thanks, Mum,' she said. 'I know it must hurt to bring it up.'

Her mother reached over and took Sarah's face in her hands. 'Sarah, I love you, and I'm here to talk about anything, at any time. I really, really hope you understand that. Don't hold back on me because you think I can't handle it. I can – whatever it is.'

Just then, the door banged open, making them both jump.

Aaron yawned as he stumbled into the kitchen. When he saw them, his eyes immediately narrowed with suspicion. 'What are you two up to?' he demanded.

'Erm, breakfast,' Sarah said, putting on her big sister face for her brother. 'You may have heard of it – first meal of the day, food after a night's fasting – it's quite common really.'

Aaron made a face at her. 'Very funny.'

Their mother smiled. 'Right, you two, that's enough. You have to be nice to each other.'

Sarah pushed back her chair. 'I need to get ready to go to the museum,' she said. She was walking towards the door when she remembered her promise to herself. She turned back and walked over to Aaron. Putting her arm round him she said, 'You are my favourite brother, though. You do know that?'

Aaron looked at her in astonishment, then his little face became wary. 'Yeah, right, I'm your *only* brother, Sarah,' he said defensively.

'Well, I only need one when he's as cool as you,' she said, then she winked at him and walked out, leaving him standing there with his mouth open.

8

Confrontation

At the bicycle stand outside the Grainger house, Sarah saw Abi, Hannah and Grace's bikes standing in a row. She could never get anywhere before them! She stood for a moment looking out at the parkland, enjoying how the grass and trees looked stiff with cold, then she turned towards the front door. She looked up at the big old house and sighed. She was not looking forward to talking to Felicity. It was just too sad having to break the news to this little girl that her spirit had passed on. And Sarah had had enough of sadness at home this week to want to deal with any more in front of her friends.

Inside, the house was warm and the volunteers were scattered about the place. Grace waved down at her from the top railing of the stairs.

'Morning, you,' she called cheerfully. 'When you're ready, could you give me a hand up in the schoolroom? I wanted to move one of the desks a bit, to make it easier for people to walk around.'

'Be with you in a sec,' Sarah called. 'I'll just go hang up my coat. Where's the other two?'

'Abi's gone to open up the mausoleum,' Grace replied, 'and Hannah is squirrelled away in a private corner –' she looked meaningfully at Sarah – 'writing some stuff.'

The writing room and the diary, Sarah thought to herself with a smile. They'd probably never see Hannah again! Her hand went up to her neck, and she checked the ribbon with the little key was still there under her shirt. She had brought her own diary with her too, and would slip into the writing room later to hide it in the desk.

Sarah made her way to the back door, beyond the kitchen stairs, and hung up her coat on the row of hooks there. As she did so, a flash of colour outside caught her eye. She moved over to the large side glass panel of the door and looked out. It was Josh, hanging about on the path that encircled the gardens.

Wonder what he's up to? she thought. Then she saw a smile flash across his face and he hurried quickly down the path, stopping suddenly to look intently at a plant. Puzzled by his strange movements, Sarah craned her neck to see more. A second flash of colour moved down the path and resolved itself into a proper outline. *Abi*, thought Sarah. She smiled to herself. *So that's his game!* She watched the look of surprise on Abi's face, then the two of them falling into step, Josh smiling the way he only ever smiled at Abi, both of them chatting easily together.

Sarah turned away and walked back to reception, before either of them spotted her. As she did, she noticed Elaine creeping out of the sitting room. She was carrying her phone and wearing her trademark smirk.

'Morning,' Sarah said, without warmth.

'Yes, and it's a *good* one,' Elaine said. She pushed her phone into her back pocket and giggled, like she had some delicious secret she was privately enjoying.

'Whatever,' Sarah muttered under her breath as she hurried across to the stairs and up to the first floor and the schoolroom.

She banged open the door. Grace was staring out the window. She spun round when Sarah walked her. 'Great. There you are,' she said, bounding towards the desks. The old school desk-and-seat was very heavy, but together they were able to hoist it over to make a bit more walking room.

'Phew! Thanks for that,' Grace said, pushing her hair off her forehead. 'That thing weighs a tonne.'

Sarah felt her phone vibrating in her pocket and went to pull it out. At the exact same moment, Grace reached her hand to her back pocket. 'Draw,' she shouted, pulling out her phone. They laughed, but then stopped abruptly as they read the text Hannah had sent to them both:

Ballroom. Now. Felicity.

'Oh no,' Sarah groaned. 'I thought we might get a few hours' quiet before this.'

Grace sighed. 'Come on, better get it over with.'

They made their way back down the stairs, meeting Abi and Josh in reception. They were looking at the tour bookings for the day.

She must be too engrossed to have heard her phone, Sarah thought.

'Hi,' Grace called. 'Abi, we're just heading into the ballroom,' she said as they walked by. 'Hannah has something important to discuss – probably wants to lecture us on some book or other,' she said with a grin.

Abi caught the looks they were sending her and her eyes widened. 'Oh sure, yeah, I'll follow you in two seconds.'

The ballroom was at the end of a corridor that led off the main reception area, in a side wing of the house. Grace and Sarah walked down the corridor quickly, then through the double doors at the end. Inside they found Hannah standing awkwardly next to Felicity, obviously waiting for them before she said anything. She looked nervous.

'Hello again, Felicity,' Grace said warmly. 'How are you?'

'I'm always the same,' Felicity said in a bored way. 'Where's the other one? Do we have to wait for her too?'

'Yep, we ghost detectives come as a job lot,' Grace joked, trying to lighten the atmosphere. It didn't work.

The door opened quietly and Abi stepped through, shutting it tightly behind her. 'Sorry I kept you waiting,' she said, nodding to Felicity.

'OK,' Felicity said, turning to them eagerly, 'how are you getting me to the performance?'

Sarah took a little step backwards. There was no way she was going to even try to do the softly softly chat – she'd be like an elephant in hobnail boots, trampling over Felicity's feelings. She knew she would. She looked hard at Abi, who she thought would be best at this sort of sensitive thing.

Abi shook her head in a tiny movement. The girls looked at one another.

'I think,' Hannah said quietly, 'you should start us off, Sarah.'

'Me again?' Sarah said, astounded. 'You're kidding. I'm not cut out for this, Hannah – you know that.'

'Yes, you are,' Hannah said, smiling at her. 'We need some plain talking now, and you're good at that.'

Abi and Grace were staring at her too, and it was clear they agreed with Hannah. Sarah glared at her friends. But they weren't going to volunteer to take her place and Felicity looked like she was about to explode with impatience, so there was nothing for it but to step forward and talk to her.

'Right, Felicity,' she began briskly, 'we have something very important that we need you to hear and understand. Right. OK. Here it is.'

'Come on, out with it!' Felicity said, rolling her eyes.

'Felicity, you are dead.'

To her left, she could hear Grace take in a sharp breath. They all looked at Felicity, but she looked completely unperturbed by this statement.

'You died,' Sarah went on, 'on the night of the show. You were on your way there, in fact. Well, maybe you were. Anyway, you went walking on a dangerous road and a car hit you and you died from your injuries. I'm really sorry to be the one to tell you all this, but you absolutely need to accept that you are dead. Once you do that, you'll be fine. There'll be no need to keep coming back for the performance because you'll understand that it's . . . over. So that's it really. You're dead, and you're a ghost now and the show is definitely over.'

When she finished her little speech, she realized her hands were trembling and her legs felt like jelly. She watched Felicity's face, waiting for the emotional storm Beryl had promised. She remembered when Louise-Anne had lost the plot in the schoolroom and she really didn't relish the prospect of another spirit tantrum.

Felicity was staring hard at her. 'Is that it?' she demanded. 'That's all you've found out?'

Sarah looked uncertainly at her friends. 'Erm . . . well, yes,' she replied.

'Well I know all *that*!' Felicity said stroppily. 'I was there, remember. I've told you again and again – all I want is to get to *Snow White*.'

'But you only care about that because you don't understand your . . . situation,' Hannah tried. 'The show is over. There is no show any more.'

Felicity crossed her arms and assumed her defiant look. 'I thought you could help me,' she said as goosebumps rose up on the girls' arms. 'You said you were here to help.'

'We are trying to help,' Sarah said. 'This is the only way we can think to help.'

'Well try *harder*,' Felicity pouted.

Sarah had had enough of this. 'Oh, I know,' she replied sarcastically, 'come out to the garden and I'll fire up my trusty time machine, then I'll transport your ghostly self back in time to six o'clock on show night, push you out of the way of that car and deliver you to the ballet school, where everyone can watch how well a *ghost girl* can dance. How about that?'

Felicity's face crumpled. She looked like she was

82

going to cry. 'Don't be so mean!' she shouted, the air shimmering dangerously round her.

Sarah stood still, her blood pounding in her ears, biting her lip and cursing herself for messing up yet again. *This is all Hannah's fault*, she thought bitterly. *I knew I couldn't do this!*

'Felicity,' Abi said as gently as she could, 'we really are doing our best here. It's just not possible to return you to that night to do your dance.'

'There has to be a way,' Felicity wailed. 'If you don't get me there, I can't get to Mia and she'll do the part instead. You have to get me to Mia!' Her face suddenly looked young and unsure again. 'At least . . . I think that's what I have to . . .' She flung her arms apart in despair and her shoulders drooped. 'Oh, what's the use?' she said sadly, then she was gone.

The girls turned to face each other, utterly perplexed by what had just happened.

'So who's Mia?' Sarah asked. 'And by the way, so-called friends, I am *not* doing that again. I'm the worst person to send to talk to a ghost. I hope you've all finally accepted that.'

'This is never going to end,' Grace said, her voice full of frustration. 'I feel like I'll be on my walking stick and Felicity will still be in my ear, asking me to get her to that damn performance!'

'You do realize that we do know who Mia is?' Hannah said suddenly.

'We do?' Sarah said, puzzled. 'I don't.'

'Remember the day we looked at the website?' Hannah prompted. 'There was a girl called Mia standing next to Simone. Her surname was Roseman.'

'Simone?' Sarah sighed. 'Great. She was completely freaked out when we asked about Felicity, now we have to ask her about someone else from the past? Wonderful. Just wonderful.'

'She's probably over the shock by now, though,' Abi said hopefully. 'Maybe it won't bother her so much.'

The girls looked at each other.

'We don't have a choice,' Hannah said quietly. 'We've nothing else to go on, do we?'

Miss Flood locked the heavy front door behind them, called a goodbye and headed off to her car. Sarah pulled her scarf tighter round her neck. It was only four o'clock, but it was already getting dark. Daniel and Jack were unlocking their bikes too and fishing out their lights from their bags.

'So will I see you at the cafe tomorrow?' Daniel asked the girls with a grin.

'What cafe?' Jack demanded, looking surprised that Daniel had had a meeting with the four girls and said nothing about it.

'Not tomorrow,' Grace said, shaking her head. 'We're only Internet nerds one Sunday a month. That's our ration!'

84

'You all met at an Internet cafe?' Jack asked in disbelief.

'We bumped into each other,' Sarah corrected him. 'Daniel was there when we arrived.'

'Oh right,' Jack said, raising an eyebrow at his friend. 'That was . . . convenient.'

Daniel blushed a little, then laughed. 'They found out my embarrassing little secret,' he joked, 'that I spend my weekends in front of a computer!'

'Oh, we're very good at finding out people's secrets, believe me,' Grace said, grinning at her friends.

'Well, see you at school then,' Daniel said. He and Jack got on their bikes and cycled off down the driveway.

Sarah, Hannah, Abi and Grace walked their bikes, delaying the moment when they would reach the gate lodge. They could see an orange light glowing down through the trees, which meant the Graingers were at home. As they passed under one of the trees, Grace reached up to pat the stone creature coiled about the lower branch.

'Remember how scared we were of these things when we first saw them?' she said, giggling to think of it.

'Yeah, crazy, isn't it?' Sarah said. 'To think we were bothered by some sculpture. We had no idea we would be facing an actual ghost not long after!'

'We did all right,' Abi said.

'I just hope we do all right this time,' Hannah said, shaking her head. 'Right now, it feels like this particular ghost has us well and truly stumped.'

'Well, here we are,' Sarah said, leaning her bike against the end wall of the gate lodge, 'back at death central.'

Her friends started laughing nervously.

'Do *not* let Simone hear you calling it that,' Hannah warned her as she stepped up to knock on the front door. 'I don't think she'd find it so funny.'

When Simone pulled open the front door, her face didn't light up like it usually did when she saw her friends standing on the doorstep. She looked unsure, almost like she was afraid of what they might say.

'Has something happened?' she asked, her voice sounding high and nervous. 'Did she flip out?'

'No, Felicity's OK,' Sarah said. She looked around. 'It's pretty cold out here, Simone, can we come in for a minute?'

'Oh right, yeah, of course. Step in,' Simone said, standing back and holding open the door.

The four girls stepped into the warmth of the front hall, but Simone didn't invite them in any further. Instead, they sat on the bench under the window opposite the reception desk. Simone twisted her hands together in her lap.

'Well?' she asked.

'It's just another question for you,' Grace began. 'A bit of the puzzle. Felicity says she knows what happened to her. So we've drawn another blank there. But she did mention someone at the –'

'Who?' Simone asked sharply.

'Mia Roseman?' Grace replied, shooting a glance at her friends.

Simone flinched and pressed her mouth into a tight line.

'Do you know her?' Grace asked.

'Not really, no,' Simone said brusquely. The girls waited for her to go on, but she didn't.

'Was she related to the owner of the academy?' Hannah asked her.

Simone nodded. 'She is Marcella Roseman's daughter.' She took a deep breath and folded her hands together. Sarah looked at Simone's hands and felt that she was trying to hide her nervousness.

But what could be making her nervous? Sarah wondered.

'She was the other star of the class,' Simone went on. 'Her mother was almost as bad as Felicity's, and they were always pitted against each other. Mrs Fenston would tell Felicity to be better than Mia, and Mrs Roseman would tell Mia she had to beat Felicity, that sort of thing. But that's all I can tell you about it.' She stood up suddenly. 'I'm really sorry, but I'm not much use to you and I've got some stuff to do for my dad, so I'd better get on with that.'

Sarah was astounded – Simone had never turfed them out like this before. She was always delighted to sit around and have a chat. The girls began to gather their things.

'Could you . . .' Hannah began. 'I mean, I know this isn't something you want to be involved in, but could you maybe introduce us to Mia? She'd remember you, right? And I think we're going to have to talk to her now, so it would be great to have you tell her that we're not completely crazy. If you could just come up to the academy and –'

'No, I can't,' Simone said, her voice sounding strained again. 'And I don't see why you need to talk to her anyway. What help can she give you? She can't change the past.'

'I know,' Hannah said, struggling to get her thoughts in order. 'But it's just, well, Felicity must be haunted by something. I mean, that's what Beryl said, isn't it? Ghosts don't haunt us, they are haunted. So if Felicity feels that she has to get to Mia, then maybe that's something to do with why she's still here.'

Simone considered this for a moment, then shook her head firmly. 'Sorry, but it's like you said – I don't want to be involved. You're the ones who did the ritual, so it's really your problem.'

Simone walked over to the door and opened it. 'I hope you can figure it out,' she said.

One by one the four girls stepped out into the

cold. They could barely speak, they were so taken aback by Simone's unusual behaviour.

'See you soon,' Grace managed as Simone closed the door and shut it with a click.

They stood on the gravel path, looking at one another in astonishment.

'Can someone tell me what just happened in there?' Abi said.

'No,' Sarah replied, 'because I have absolutely no idea. Seriously, did some weird ghost just steal Simone's body and that wasn't really her?'

'Beats me,' Abi said, shaking her head.

'This whole thing just keeps getting weirder,' Grace said with a sigh. 'I feel like I've no idea what's even going on.'

'Something has rattled her,' Hannah said thoughtfully. 'I think there's something she's not telling us.'

'Like what?' Abi asked.

Hannah shrugged. 'I don't know,' she said, 'but she's not behaving like normal, is she?'

'Normal?' Sarah said, whistling through her teeth. 'At the moment, Simone and normal are two ships passing in the night. Destined never to meet.'

Hannah arched an eyebrow at her friend. 'Well, that's one way to put it.'

Grace shook her head and scuffed the toe of her Converse against the gravel. 'It's like she's not our friend any more,' she said, sounding hurt.

Sarah put her arm round Grace. Hannah looked over at the gate lodge one last time, then turned towards the bikes. 'I'd say we're pretty much on our own with this one,' she said. 'Somehow or other we have to find out what's bothering Felicity, and after that we can find out what's bothering Simone.'

9

Nasty Tricks

On Monday morning, Grace and Hannah met up near their houses as usual and walked to school together. As they neared the school there was a sudden crack of thunder and they were pelted with hailstones.

'Ouch, those things hurt,' Grace gasped as she sprinted towards the gates. She raced through the yard and then burst through the door into the cloakroom, Hannah hard on her heels. They collapsed in laughter as soon as they were safely inside.

'Wow,' said Hannah, shaking hailstones out of her hair, 'my face is stinging from where they hit.'

They were pulling off scarves and coats when Sarah came hurtling through the door, her red hair dotted with hailstones too.

'Seriously, what is it with the weather? Can't we just have snow for Christmas like they do in books?' she said, dropping her bag to the floor and giving her head a vigorous shake, like a dog after a bath.

'We still might,' said Grace hopefully. 'Then we can sing about snow to our heart's content.'

'Of course, yeah, because that's what I dream of every December,' Sarah replied with a grin, 'swanning about singing songs about snow. Naturally.'

Grace poked her in the ribs and started to sing, '*I'm dreaming of a white Christmas . . .*'

Sarah put her hands over her ears and groaned loudly as Hannah burst out laughing. They were interrupted by Tiffany putting her head round the door. She rolled her eyes when she saw their antics.

'Very mature, girls,' she drawled.

Sarah lowered her hands and stared at Chrissy's friend. 'Was there something you wanted, Tiffany?' she asked the smaller blonde girl. 'Has your leader sent you to deliver a message or something?'

'Or something,' Tiffany said with a mean grin, narrowing her eyes. 'I just thought you lot might be interested to find out what kind of girl your friend Abi really is.'

Sarah, Grace and Hannah were immediately defensive.

'What's that supposed to mean?' Sarah demanded. She felt angry at the thought of the Clones picking on Abi in any way. Chrissy's promise to get Abi back for what happened on the museum's opening night flashed through her mind.

Tiffany shrugged her shoulders and laughed. 'You'll find out soon enough,' she said, then left.

The girls looked at one another nervously.

'I don't think I even want to know what she's on about,' Grace said anxiously. She reached into her schoolbag and grabbed her phone. It wasn't meant to be used on school grounds, but this was an emergency. She switched it on and texted Abi:

Where are you?

A moment later, her phone beeped.

Just at school gates. Why?

Grace typed back:

See you in cloakroom when you get here.

A few minutes later the door pushed open and Abi stepped into the cloakroom. Sarah looked out at the patch of sky revealed by the open door. The hailstones had stopped, but the clouds were very low and very dark.

Abi smiled at her three friends. 'Hey, a welcoming committee for little old me? You shouldn't have.' Then she noticed their worried faces and she stopped smiling. 'What is it?' she asked.

'We don't know,' Grace said, 'but Tiffany was just here and she said something about us finding out what kind of a girl you are. I've no idea what she's talking about, but we were a bit worried about you. Have the Clones been annoying you?'

'No, not at all,' Abi said, looking mystified. 'I can't think what she meant by that.'

'Well, they're not going to get you alone, if that's what they're thinking,' Hannah said darkly. 'We'll be at your side all day.'

Abi smiled gratefully at her. 'Jeez, Hannah, I didn't know you could sound so scary. Come on, you guys,' she said, hanging up her coat and grabbing her bag, 'they're probably just trying to rattle us, as usual. Chrissy is dead set on getting us out of the museum, so it's probably more fake complaints or something. Let's get to class and forget about her.'

The girls picked up their bags and headed out to the corridor. As they walked along, the other kids were grinning and talking behind their hands. They all seemed to be looking at Abi. They walked in silence, surrounded by waves of giggles and whispers.

'Is it just me or is something definitely going on?' Sarah said.

Before anyone could answer her, one of the boys shouted out, 'Hey, Abi, will you give me a kiss?' The corridor exploded in laughter. Abi blushed fiercely, but she couldn't tell who had said it. And she certainly couldn't think why whoever it was had shouted it at her.

The girls rounded the corner on to the corridor their classrooms were on. The school noticeboard was on the wall at the bottom of the corridor, and there were about fifteen kids gathered round it, all giggling and talking at once.

It was Sarah who saw it first. Her hand flew to her mouth as she realized what Chrissy had done. There, pinned to the noticeboard, was a photograph of Abi and Josh in the garden at the museum. They were walking side by side, close together, and smiling shyly at each other.

Elaine! Sarah thought with a jolt of realization. *That little snake. That's what she was doing.*

The kids in front of the noticeboard parted suddenly and someone called out, 'Ooh, Abi, nice photo. You and Josh Fitzsimons, who would have thought?'

Abi's face went from red to white in a split second. She pushed forward to look at the noticeboard, Hannah and Grace looking over her shoulders to see what it was. When she saw the photo, Abi gasped like she'd been punched in the stomach. Sarah could feel the anger shaking through her. Under the photo it said:

Congratulations to Abi and Josh for being in love. You thought the museum was all hard work? Wrong! These two lovebirds are having a lot of fun!

Sarah looked over at Hannah and Grace – their eyes were wide in disbelief as they stared at the photo.

'How could she –' Hannah began but she didn't get any further. Chrissy, Elaine, Tiffany and Sophie appeared on the corridor behind them, and there was no mistaking the look of pure triumphant delight in Chrissy's eyes. The Clones were grinning and giggling, bunched up on either side of Chrissy. Abi was still standing motionless, like she'd been robbed of all ability to move.

'Oh hey, Abi,' Chrissy called in a voice sticky with sweetness. 'Well done you on bagging such a gorgeous boy. It must be your American way with boys that won him over, was it?'

Standing there, in front of everybody, Abi suddenly burst into tears. Then she turned and ran, with everyone staring after her, open-mouthed. Chrissy and her friends started to laugh loudly, and Sarah thought her head was going to burst with anger. Hannah and Grace took off after Abi, but Sarah stood her ground.

'You are a horrible person,' she shouted wildly at Chrissy. 'And you,' she said swinging round to the knot of girls in front of the noticeboard, 'are no better. Abi and Josh are just friends,' she roared, loud enough for everyone to hear. 'Now grow up, the lot of you.' Then she turned and ran after Abi, hearing Chrissy's laugh echoing in her head. At the other end of the corridor, she could see Hannah's blonde hair disappearing into the toilets after their friend.

As she raced past the open door to her classroom, Josh stepped out and grabbed her arm. 'What's going on?' he asked her, looking perplexed. 'Why are you shouting about me and Abi being friends?'

Sarah bit her lip. If he didn't know about the photo, she didn't want to be the one to alert him to it. She should run back and grab it before he could even know about it. Her eyes flicked down the corridor to where her classmates were still gathered at the noticeboard. Josh followed her gaze and saw Chrissy looking very pleased with herself, and Tiffany, Elaine and Sophie all laughing behind their hands.

'What's she done?' he demanded instantly, not letting go of Sarah's arm.

I am seriously unlucky, Sarah thought. There was nothing for it but to tell him – he obviously wasn't going to let her go until he found out.

'She got you two back,' Sarah said, nodding her head towards Chrissy. 'There's a photo on the board of you and Abi. Elaine took it at the museum.'

Josh didn't say a word, but she could feel his whole body tense up.

'It's just a stupid, mean trick,' Sarah said with a sigh, 'but Abi's really upset.' She looked down towards Chrissy and her friends, then back at Josh. 'Chrissy really knows how to get to a person, I'll give her that.'

'Where's Abi now?' Josh asked her.

'In the toilets. I have to go.'

Josh nodded at her, then turned to go down the corridor. 'Tell Abi it's gone,' he said, walking towards the noticeboard.

Sarah hurried to the toilets and went inside. She found Hannah and Grace comforting Abi, who was crying against the hand-dryer. Her face was all blotchy and she looked utterly miserable. Sarah felt sick to see her friend so upset. She went straight over and hugged her tightly.

'Don't let her get to you,' she said, rubbing Abi's back. 'She's a witch, that girl.'

'But . . . how did she even get that picture?' Abi wailed.

'I know exactly how,' Sarah said. Hannah and Grace looked at her in surprise. 'Elaine took it on her phone when Josh and you were walking in the garden. Remember, he met you on the path after you opened the mausoleum on Saturday? I saw Elaine come out of the sitting room with her phone in her hand, looking like the cat that got the cream. I didn't realize then what she'd done, but it had to be her.'

Abi raised her head to look at her friends. 'No way. You're saying she was actually *spying* on me to get something she could use against me?' She looked shocked at the thought.

'She did say she'd get you back,' Grace said grimly.

'She and Chrissy were determined to make you and Josh pay – but this is something else, even by their standards.'

Abi groaned into her hands. 'What if Miss Flood saw it? What if she believes it and kicks me out of the museum?'

'That is *not* going to happen,' Sarah said firmly. 'Miss Flood knows what Chrissy is like. She'll see this for what it is.'

'I'm just so embarrassed,' Abi whispered, her voice breaking. 'How can I go back out there?'

Sarah turned her round and lifted her chin. 'You can go back out there, Abigail Worthy, because you're a wonderful person and have never treated anyone as badly as Chrissy and Elaine just treated you. You can go out there because you know what you did and didn't do. You have to show them all that it's a pile of nonsense by holding your head up high and ignoring those stupid girls who want to make a deal of it. Anyway, they're just jealous.'

Abi nodded at Sarah, but her eyes still filled with tears. Sarah took her hands in hers. 'Abi, remember what she did to me – saying that stuff about my dad? I wanted the ground to swallow me up, but I had to just face her down. That's all you can do now.'

Abi took a deep breath and rubbed her eyes with the back of her hand. She breathed deeply again and looked at Sarah. 'I know you're right,' she said quietly.

'The picture is gone now,' Sarah said steadily.

'Thank you,' Abi replied.

'It's not me you have to thank,' Sarah said. She wasn't sure how Abi would take the news that Josh knew, but it was better to give it to her straight. 'Josh went to take it down.'

Abi swallowed hard. 'He saw it too?' she said, fighting back more tears.

'Yeah, he did,' Sarah said, 'and he was just as angry as me. He was worried about you actually, and he went off to get rid of it. So it's gone.'

Hannah cleared her throat and said gently, 'Abi, I know this is really hard, but we're late. Class will have started now and they'll be wondering where we are.'

Abi nodded and dragged her hand across her eyes again. 'Two seconds,' she said. She grabbed some tissue and ran the water from the tap, dabbing at her face until she looked a bit less blotchy. Then she threw back her shoulders, stuck out her chin and smiled weakly at her friends. 'OK, ready as I'll ever be.'

They walked out of the toilets and made their way down to the door of the classroom. Sarah knew exactly how Abi was feeling – it was really awful when Chrissy got her hooks into you – so she was really proud to see her friend squaring up to the world and refusing to back down.

'That's the spirit, Abi,' she whispered in Abi's ear as she opened the classroom door and they prepared to get on with the rest of their day.

10

The Roseman Academy

The next day was Tuesday and the school was only open for a half day – or a teachers' shopping day, as Grace called it. It was their best chance to get some time to go to the ballet school and try to talk to Mia.

'Do you think she'll talk to us?' Grace asked for the tenth time as they unlocked their bikes in the schoolyard.

Hannah shook her head. 'We don't know, Grace, I keep telling you. It's just that we have to try it, to see if we can find out anything else that might help us to help Felicity.'

'This is going to be a disaster, I can feel it,' Sarah said glumly as she climbed on to her saddle. 'We're going to walk up to a complete stranger and say, *Hey, can you help us to put an angry little ghost to rest? Oh and by the way, we're not crazy. Honest.*' She pulled on her hat and made a face. 'If this Mia doesn't call the police, we'll be doing well.'

'Or the men in white coats,' Grace said with a

grin. 'We might be carted off to some home for the bewildered before we know what's happening!'

'Well, now I'm not at *all* nervous,' Hannah said drily. 'Thanks, you two.'

'Are you ready, Abi?' Sarah asked. Abi nodded at her. She hadn't been her usual self since she'd seen that photograph yesterday. Sarah knew they just had to give her time to get over it.

'Come on, let's go see the dancing divas,' Grace called over her shoulder as she cycled towards the gates.

It took about twenty-five minutes to cycle to the academy and their faces were raw with cold by the time they got there. When they'd cycled up the short driveway, Sarah was surprised – it wasn't what she'd expected. It was actually just a big house, with a long, low building attached on one side that reminded her of the assembly hall in school. Above the front door of the house it said MAIN ENTRANCE, and above the double doors of the hall it said, AUDITORIUM ENTRANCE. It wasn't flashy or modern at all.

'This isn't what I thought a dancing academy would look like,' she remarked to the others as they parked their bikes.

Hannah nodded. 'My cousin used to go here and she told me they are always fund-raising because they'd love a new space, but so far they've never made enough money.'

The four girls walked up to the main entrance

and peeped inside. Apart from the photo of her when she was ten years old, they had no idea what Mia Roseman would look like now.

'So how will we do this?' Grace asked.

They looked at each other uncertainly.

'Well, I suppose we'd better go inside, for starters,' Hannah said.

They stepped into the hallway and looked around. There was a sign for the office on the left-hand side and stairs curved up on their right, leading to the first floor. Photographs adorned the walls of the hallway.

'We can look for her in the photos,' Hannah said, happy to have some sort of help. 'Hopefully there's a newer one of her, so at least we'll know what she looks like.'

They started working their way down the hall, examining each of the photos in turn. There came the sound of footsteps from outside and a tall girl stepped through the door. She was wearing normal clothes, but her hair was pulled back in a ballerina's bun and she was carrying a sports bag. She walked quickly in the direction of the office, then stopped abruptly when she saw the four girls. Sarah looked up – it was Sophie, one of Chrissy's friends. Sarah turned fully to look at her and crossed her arms, giving Sophie a look that could wither flowers. Normally, Sophie would be equally determined, but this time she looked a bit scared. Her eyes flicked from Sarah to Abi to Hannah and then to Grace, and she took a step backwards. Then another.

'Well, that's very interesting,' Sarah remarked. 'Without the rest of your gang, you're suddenly not so brave, is that it?' She glared at Sophie.

'Are you hoping to take photos of us on your phone too – just like Elaine?' Grace asked in a voice that was distinctly icy.

Sophie looked directly at Abi and her face went red, then she suddenly turned on her heel and ran out of the house. The girls stared after her in surprise.

'Well, that's a turn up for the books,' Hannah said. 'I never thought she'd be such a scaredy-cat when she was on her own.'

'My dad says all bullies are terrified underneath,' Abi said quietly.

'He might have a point,' Hannah said, still staring at the door through which Sophie had escaped.

'Look!' Grace interrupted suddenly. 'There's Felicity!'

Her three friends swung round in fright, fearing the worst.

'Where?' Sarah almost shouted, looking about frantically.

'Right there,' Grace said, pointing at the wall near the office. Hanging beside the door to the office was a photograph of Felicity in a beautiful ballet costume, her arms raised above her head.

'Seriously, Grace,' Sarah said, clutching her chest, 'you nearly gave me a heart attack!'

'What? Why?' Grace asked, puzzled.

'I thought she was here, as in the real Felicity. I mean, the kind of real Felicity, I mean – oh, you know what I mean. The actual her!'

'Oh sorry,' Grace said with a grin. 'That's why you guys looked so strange. No, I just meant the picture.'

They went over and read the caption underneath: *Felicity Fenston, who was a student here for five years. Sadly missed by all her friends.*

'Look at that pose she's striking,' Grace said admiringly, 'she must have been so good at ballet. I bet I couldn't do that no matter how hard I tried.'

'Go on then, give it a go,' Sarah said, daring her.

Grace immediately went up on her toes and stretched up her arms, with a pouty look on her face. Her friends burst out laughing. Suddenly, the office door swung open and a tall, thin woman dressed all in black stepped out.

'*What* is going on here?' she demanded.

The girls froze.

'*Well?*' she said loudly.

'We . . . I'm . . . sorry,' Grace stammered. 'I was just trying to copy the pose in the photo.'

The woman looked her up and down from the toes of her Converse to the top of her head. 'Oh really?' was all she said, but it was very clear that what she meant was, 'Only in your dreams will you ever achieve *that* pose!'

Grace blushed and looked down at the floor, feeling very small and stupid all of a sudden.

'Are you here for a reason?' the woman went on, still in that cold, clipped voice. 'I'm Marcella Roseman. I own this academy, so if you're looking to join you need to talk to me.'

The four friends looked at one another. How in the world could they talk to this woman about Felicity? It was Abi who managed to speak first.

'We were hoping we could talk to Mia actually,' she said in a quiet voice.

'Mia?' the woman said suspiciously. 'Why do you need to speak to my daughter? I've never seen you before. You're not friends of hers.'

'No, we're not,' Abi went on, doing her best to meet the woman's stern eye. 'But we just needed to talk to her about . . . something. It's nothing really, just part of a . . . sort of . . . project we're working on.'

The woman stared hard at Abi and didn't look at all convinced by this explanation. 'Project?' she demanded.

'Erm, well, yes, just a sort of local-history project,' Abi ploughed on, 'that touches on . . . dancing and . . . Felicity Fenston.'

The woman's eyebrows shot up her forehead at the mention of Felicity's name. 'I can't think why a local-history project would need to involve little Felicity,' she said sharply, sounding very suspicious now. 'I'm going to ask you to leave,' she said, moving towards them with her arms out, like she was herding sheep. 'Please leave. I don't want you upsetting Mia with talk of things that are in the past.'

'But we wouldn't want to upset –' Abi began, but it was no use. Marcella Roseman had obviously decided these four strangers were up to no good and there was no way they were going to get past her to Mia. She ushered them down the hallway, past all the photos, then out through the front door.

'I would advise you to stay away from here,' she said, 'and stay away from my daughter.' She shut the door with a bang, leaving the four girls standing outside, shell-shocked by how quickly it had all happened.

'That went well,' Sarah remarked drily.

Grace shook her head. 'I give up,' she said tiredly. 'Every time we mention Felicity, we get shown the door. First Simone, now this creepy woman puts us out. We just can't help Felicity. I think we'll just have to accept that and tell her we're sorry.'

Abi reached over and rubbed Grace's shoulder. 'We can't give up yet,' she said gently.

'I don't think it's our fault,' Sarah said, ready to agree with Grace. 'We've tried and tried, but we can't figure out what help she needs and we can't get anyone to help us figure it out, so here we are, helpless!'

'I know,' Abi replied, 'but she's so young and so . . . lost. There must be another way we can get to talk to Mia.'

'*Pssst.*'

Abi looked around, confused. 'Did you guys hear that noise?' she asked.

'*Over here,*' a voice whispered.

The girls looked over towards the corner of the house, and there, peeping her head round, was a tall, slender girl of about sixteen. She was wearing a ballet rehearsal costume of leotard and tights, and her pale skin looked almost translucent. The girls stared at her.

'Is it another ghost?' Abi asked faintly.

The girl beckoned to them, then disappeared from view. Sarah looked at her friends and shrugged. 'I guess we have to follow her,' she said.

They walked round the corner and saw that the side-gate had been left open. They went through it into a garden and saw the girl standing behind a tree. She beckoned them again, indicating that they were to follow her. Then she turned and left the garden through another small gate. They moved quickly and quietly, following the apparition to a neat grass path that was shielded on both sides by an avenue of rhododendron trees. Halfway down the avenue, the girl was standing, waiting for them.

'Is it really another ballerina ghost?' Sarah whispered. She was wondering how many young dancers had managed to meet an early end in the town, and feeling very glad she'd always had two left feet.

'Only one way to find out,' Hannah said and she walked on ahead, the other three falling in step behind her.

When they reached the girl, she smiled at them. Sarah could see goosebumps along her arms and her lips were bluish with the cold. She shivered and clutched her arms about her for warmth. *She's definitely flesh and blood,* Sarah thought with relief.

'Hi,' the girl said through chattering teeth. 'I'm Mia.'

11

Rivals

There was a silence as the girls stared at Mia and Mia stared at the girls with great curiosity. Sarah felt sorry for her, shivering in the cold of the afternoon.

'Right, first things first,' Sarah said firmly, 'you can't stand talking to us like that. Here, take my coat.' She unbuttoned her coat and started to take it off.

'Oh no, that's not necessary,' Mia said quickly. 'You'll freeze. Leave it on.'

'I've got a warm jumper on,' Sarah said, dismissing Mia's protests. 'Come on, throw it on you.'

Mia smiled gratefully at her. 'Thanks. I am cold.' She pulled on Sarah's coat and snuggled herself down into it, digging her hands deep into the pockets. She looked at the four friends. 'I heard you inside, talking to my mother. Why do you need to see me?' She was obviously very interested to hear why four girls she'd never met and didn't know had come looking for her. She glanced back up the grass path, towards the house. 'I don't have long,' she said. 'I didn't let Mum know I was leaving.'

Sarah, Hannah, Grace and Abi exchanged a look. They knew there was absolutely nothing for it now but to plunge in with the truth and hope Mia didn't run away screaming. There was no time to lead her in gently – it was going to have to be the blunt facts of the matter.

Hannah cleared her throat. 'Mia, my name is Hannah,' she began, 'and this is Sarah, Abi and Grace.'

Mia nodded at them and smiled. 'Nice to meet you,' she said.

'Well, the thing is,' Hannah continued, taking a deep breath, 'we have been visited by Felicity Fenston. I know she's not alive,' she said quickly, seeing the startled look on Mia's face, 'but she's still around. She can't rest in peace and she came to us to ask for our help.'

Mia's mouth slowly dropped open and she looked from one girl to the next, utter disbelief on her face. 'Are you talking about . . . ghosts?' she said quietly.

'Yes, we are,' Hannah replied. 'I know it sounds strange and, let's face it, crazy, but it is true. I can't tell you how, but ghosts who need help come to us and we try to . . . help.'

She paused, to let that sink in. Mia was shaking her head, trying very hard to keep up with Hannah's incredible story.

'You really believe this, don't you?' she said at last.

'We didn't beforehand,' Sarah interrupted. 'I thought it was a pile of nonsense. But there's no way we'd be standing here saying all this to a complete stranger and making idiots of ourselves if it wasn't true. Why would we track you down and say all this?'

Mia cocked her head to one side and regarded Sarah carefully. 'All right, that would be even weirder, I grant you. OK, let's say you are able to talk to dead people and solve their problems – what's this got to do with Felicity? And with me?'

'We're not entirely sure,' Hannah admitted. 'All we can tell you is that Felicity came to us for help. She said she had to get to the *Snow White* performance – it was all she would talk about. We've tried telling her that it's long over and we can't get her there, but then she said she had to get to Mia. Something is stopping her from moving on, but she won't tell us and we can't figure out what it is, so we're sort of . . . Well, this is a shot in the dark, I know, but we just thought you might be able to tell us about her, why she might want to see you or do that last dance. Anything at all might be helpful.'

Mia threw back her head and laughed, then clamped her hand over her mouth, looking almost surprised at herself for her own reaction. 'Sorry,' she gasped, 'but that really does sound like Felicity.

I think I'm starting to believe you, but this is just so far out there my brain can't process it at all.'

'I know,' Sarah replied with a grin. 'We will be hoping you keep this strictly to yourself. So far only us and Simone know about any of this stuff, and we'd like to keep it that way.'

Mia looked sharply at Sarah. 'Did you say Simone?' she demanded. 'Simone who? Grainger?'

'Yes,' Sarah said, nodding. 'She's a friend of ours.'

Mia's face changed and she looked a bit less friendly than she had up to now. 'So is Simone involved in this?' she asked with an edge to her voice.

'Not as such,' Hannah answered. 'We did ask her about Felicity, but she just said she didn't know her much and couldn't help us.'

'Didn't know her?' Mia repeated, looking surprised. 'That's odd.'

'Why?' Hannah asked quickly. 'Did you all know each other?'

'Yes, we did,' Mia replied. 'Simone was my best friend at ballet. Felicity wasn't a friend as such, but we knew each other well.'

'Wait a second,' Sarah said, holding up her hand. 'You're saying Simone was your *best friend*?' She looked around at her three friends. 'Simone didn't say anything like that to us. She made it sound like she barely knew Felicity, or you.'

'Did she now?' Mia said drily. 'I can't say I'm surprised by that.'

'Hang on,' Hannah said, rubbing her temples, 'now *my* brain is hurting. Mia, can you please start at the beginning and fill us in on what the story was between you three?'

Mia sighed and glanced again towards the house. 'OK,' she said wearily. 'Simone was my best friend in ballet. Felicity was a brilliant dancer, but she and I didn't get along. It was our mothers, really. Her mother pushed her so hard to be the best and because I was good too she saw me as the main one to beat.' Mia shrugged her shoulders. 'My mother wasn't much better. As the daughter of the owner, I've always been expected to be the star in the class. I hated the way they pushed us to compete like serious rivals, but it's just the way it was. Anyway, Simone and I hit it off from day one. Felicity was wrapped up in her practice and the big future she was going to have in the limelight at some top ballet company.'

Mia stopped and bit her lip.

'Could you and Felicity have been friends if your mothers had been different?' Hannah asked gently.

'I don't know,' Mia said. 'I don't think Felicity liked me at all. She was pretty hard on me. I've always been a bit shy and don't like fights or anything like that, but Felicity could be really mean and cutting. Even as a ten-year-old!' Mia's face reddened and she looked unsure. 'I don't like to say this stuff,' she said, 'because it's, you know, speaking ill of the dead.'

'I understand,' Hannah said, nodding. 'What about Simone? Why aren't you two friends any more?'

'I wish I knew,' Mia replied. 'After the accident and the funeral, Simone gave up ballet and stopped talking to me. She just sort of disappeared. She started doing home-schooling with her dad and spending all her time in the lodge. I tried to get her to talk to me, but she just shut me out. After a while, I gave up. She made it clear she didn't want to know me.'

'That's really strange,' Grace said. 'That doesn't sound like Simone. I'd love to know what was going through her head.'

'Yeah, me too,' Mia said with a sad smile. 'But what I also can't understand,' she went on, 'is why Felicity would mention me. She didn't like me, so why would she want anything to do with me? I honestly have no idea.' She looked thoughtful for a moment, then her expression changed again. 'Listen to me,' she said, as if she was talking to herself, 'talking about a ghost Felicity as if it was normal.'

'I know that feeling,' Sarah remarked.

'But why would she come back now, years later?' Mia asked.

'That we don't know,' Hannah said. 'Maybe it's because it's the anniversary of the concert and her death?'

'Yeah, maybe,' Mia said absently. 'Or maybe she felt she'd found the right people to talk to, you know, someone closer to her own age.'

For some reason that idea made Sarah feel uncomfortable. She looked at her friends and could tell they hadn't thought about it that way before either. It was like suggesting Felicity had been waiting for them, like she knew some day they would come. Sarah felt a little shiver run down her back.

'Mia,' Abi said, 'is there anything at all you can think of that might explain why Felicity isn't at peace? Like maybe her relationship with her mother? Or something she was meant to do and didn't? Or anything about how she died and why she was on that road and not at the performance like she should have been?' She stopped and smiled ruefully. 'As you can see, all we have at the moment are questions and no answers.'

Mia shook her head slowly. 'It's beyond me. I didn't know her well enough to know much about her life. All she did was ballet. That was it. And sometimes she took her frustrations out on me because I was an easy target and never stood up for myself. That's all I ever knew of her. I've no idea what she was doing the night she died, or why she went off down that road.' She stopped and looked thoughtful for a moment. 'To be honest, it makes sense to me that she came to you talking about dancing *Snow White* because ballet was her life. It was absolutely everything.'

Sarah racked her brains, trying to think of some clever question that could lead to a helpful answer, but she was drawing a blank – as they always seemed to when it came to Felicity. She was just about to ask about how Simone and Felicity got on when Mia suddenly straightened up and pulled off her coat. She handed it to Sarah.

'You know, I . . . I have to leave. This is all just too much for me. It's crazy.'

'Please,' Sarah said quickly, 'will you take my number and get in touch if you think of anything else?'

Mia hesitated, but then she relented. 'Fine, look, put my number in your phone and text me yours later.'

Sarah pulled her phone out of her bag and tapped in the number Mia called out.

'Can we talk to you again, if we need to?' Hannah asked.

'Maybe,' Mia said, looking now like she was desperate to get away from them. 'I have to think about all this. I just don't know what to make of it.' She turned and ran lightly down the length of the grass path, darting through the gate at the end and back towards the house.

'We just keep spreading the joy, don't we?' Sarah said, watching Mia disappear through the trees.

'And now someone we don't even know knows our secret,' Abi said dubiously. 'That makes me very nervous.'

'Why?' Grace asked. 'You don't think she'd rat us out and tell anyone about this?'

Abi shrugged. 'I've no idea what her reaction will be when she thinks it over. Let's face it, it has to be the strangest conversation she's ever had in her life. We don't know what effect it will have on her.'

Sarah chewed her lip – Abi was right, this could all blow up in their faces. She felt sick at the idea of the whole town laughing at the 'ghost detectives'.

'I still think we've done the right thing,' Hannah said. 'We have a lost little ten-year-old girl and we have to help her. Somehow.'

'Yeah, well, if we don't end up with four imprisoned twelve-year-olds as a result,' Sarah said grimly.

'You're such a drama queen, Sarah Forde,' Hannah teased her.

'So what have we found out about Felicity, then?' Grace asked.

'We know that she knows she's dead,' Hannah replied, 'so that's not the problem. We know she's obsessed with the *Snow White* performance, and that Mia is mixed up in that in her head. We also know that Simone doesn't want to talk about Mia or Felicity, but did know them both. Plus, we now know that Felicity had a bit of a mean streak too. And I think we know that Felicity doesn't really know why she's here either – I'd guess she's about as confused as us right now.'

'And that's it?' Grace said.

'Unless I'm missing something, then, yeah, that's it,' Hannah replied.

'Not a lot, is it?' Grace said with a frown. 'Do you think we're going to fail on only our second ever ghost?'

At the exact same moment, Hannah said, 'No,' and Sarah said, 'Yes.' They grinned at each other.

'Well, that about sums up this whole Felicity thing,' Grace said, giggling. 'We haven't a clue, do we?'

12

The Ballroom

On Saturday, things were a little strained at the museum. Abi was ignoring Chrissy and Elaine, and she couldn't bring herself to look Josh in the eye. He was being very nice and gentle whenever he spoke to her, but he kept looking at her anxiously, obviously worried about how upset she was. Sarah, Grace and Hannah were worried about her too, but they were trying to act normal. Chrissy and Elaine didn't seem bothered at all – they were full of smiles and chat, pleased with their handiwork in getting revenge on Abi.

It's going to be another long day, Sarah thought to herself.

During her lunch break, Sarah decided to go to the writing room and write a bit in her diary. She sneaked in there, bringing her sandwich and drink with her. It was quiet and peaceful on her own inside – much better than walking on eggshells among the volunteers outside. She got her diary out of the bottom drawer of the writing desk and looped the ribbon over her head. She slid the tiny key into the diary's lock and opened it. Then she looked back over her entries so far – it was a weird story, and sometimes she still couldn't believe it was her life now.

Suddenly, Sarah became aware of a chill in the room and she looked up. Felicity was standing close by, watching her. Sarah gasped in surprise, then calmed herself. 'Hi, Felicity,' she said quietly. 'Have you been there long?'

'What are you doing?' Felicity asked nosily.

Sarah quickly shut and locked the diary. 'Just writing up some stuff,' she said offhandedly.

'Is that your secret diary?' Felicity said with amusement in her voice.

'It's none of your business,' Sarah said sharply.

Felicity stuck out her tongue at her. 'Fine, have it your way,' she said sulkily.

Sarah remembered the other times she'd got it wrong with the young ghost and decided she'd try to do better this time. 'Hey, I'm sorry,' she said, smiling. 'It is a diary and I just want to keep it private, that's all.'

'That's OK,' Felicity replied with a shrug. 'This place is nice,' she said suddenly, looking around. 'So quiet, isn't it?'

'Yeah, that's why I like hiding out in here,' Sarah admitted.

'What are you hiding from?' Felicity asked.

'Well, today things are a bit hard because Chrissy – she's the girl with the long black hair – she played a seriously nasty trick on Abi and Abi's really upset about it.' Sarah shook her head. 'You wouldn't believe how mean Chrissy can be.'

Felicity looked a bit uncomfortable. 'What did she do?' she asked.

'Her friend took a photo on her phone of Abi and Josh talking in the garden, then Chrissy printed it out and pinned it up on the noticeboard in school. She wrote underneath that they were in love. Abi is so embarrassed about it.'

Felicity looked shocked, then angry, and Sarah felt the goosebumps rise up on her arms. 'That's awful,' Felicity said, looking like she was close to tears. 'I mean, that's not just a trick, that's really, properly horrible.'

'Tell me about it,' Sarah said unhappily. 'Abi is such a great friend, I hate to see her getting hurt.' She looked up at Felicity and could see that the ballerina was really upset by the story about Chrissy. She felt it was a good time to change the subject.

'So how are you feeling about everything now?' she asked, as gently as she could. 'Is getting to *Snow White* still everything to you?'

Felicity's little face looked sad. 'It's all I can think about,' she admitted, 'but I wish I could change that.'

'How do you mean?' Sarah asked, confused.

'It's hard to explain,' Felicity said with a sigh.

'It's like I'm in a fog or something. My mind is just on *Snow White*, but I keep feeling there's something else I should be thinking about.' She shrugged helplessly. 'I'm really not sure what's going on, or why I'm here,' she said in a small voice.

Sarah couldn't believe she was talking to her so honestly. *Don't blow this, Sarah*, she willed herself.

'I know it's frustrating, Felicity,' Sarah went on, 'but we are still trying to figure it out. There has to be a way to help you find peace, and we want to do that.'

The ghost looked at her and gave a half-smile. 'Thank you,' she whispered. 'I can be such a pain at times, I know. My mum always used to tell me that. But you are all really nice. I hope I haven't upset you or anything.'

'No, don't worry about things like that,' Sarah said quickly, eager to reassure her. She seemed so young and vulnerable when she was talking like this – it made Sarah want to protect her, to make everything better for her.

Felicity gave another sad smile, then the air started to shimmer and she left. Sarah took a deep breath and steadied her breathing. She could still feel the little girl's sadness, and it made her want to cry. Instead, she put away her diary, tidied up her lunch things and went off to find the girls, so she could tell them about Felicity's visit and what she'd said.

* * *

'Oh jeez, poor Felicity!' Abi said, her face crumpled with worry.

'I know,' Sarah said, 'I felt like weeping myself, which doesn't happen very often.'

Hannah smiled at her. 'Well, if she melted your heart of stone, she really must have been upset.'

'She was, Hannah,' Sarah said. 'She wants to move on, but she said she can't think clearly enough to find out what's wrong in the first place.'

'So how can *we* find out, then?' Grace asked. She looked at her watch. 'It's half three,' she said, 'do you think we should go early and try Simone just one more time?'

'What about Felicity's mother?' Hannah asked suddenly.

'You mean, try to find her and ask her about this?' Grace asked, sounding shocked at the idea.

'I'd rather pull out my own toenails,' Sarah said, feeling every bit as shocked as Grace.

'Well I'm not saying I *want* to,' Hannah replied defensively, 'but maybe Felicity hasn't forgiven her mother for pushing her so hard. I mean, we did first meet her in the nursery, remember? Could that be the missing link in all this?'

'If it is, it can stay missing,' Sarah said, folding her arms. 'I can't think of anything worse than calling her mother out of the blue and telling her we're in touch with her daughter, who died six years ago and still hasn't found peace. Come on,

Hannah, that's not something we could actually do.'

Hannah looked a bit put out by Sarah's reaction. 'I don't hear you coming up with solutions, Sarah,' she retorted. 'At least I'm trying.'

'I do have an idea, as it happens,' Sarah replied.

Her friends looked at her in surprise. 'You do? Well out with it,' Grace said impatiently.

'It's just that, talking to her today, I think the only thing we can do is stage the performance. That has to be the answer. If it's all she can think about, then let her dance it and see if that unblocks the rest of the problem for her.'

Abi, Hannah and Grace looked unsure. Sarah knew it probably sounded a bit lame as an idea, but it was definitely better than opening any more cans of worms with people from Felicity's old life.

'Stage it how exactly?' Hannah asked.

'I haven't thought about the details,' Sarah admitted, 'but if we can make her believe she's doing the dance at last, then maybe that would help.'

There was silence as the girls digested this, then Abi spoke. 'I think Sarah's probably right,' she said. 'We've hit a wall with everything else. All we really know is that she wants to be Snow White, so if we can give her that, it might just work to let her mind find rest.'

'I suppose so,' Grace said uncertainly. 'But we'll need to think carefully about how we could do it.'

'What if –' Sarah began, but she was interrupted by the appearance of Jack.

'There you are – all huddled together as usual,' he said. 'There's a visitor at the desk and she wants you lot to give her the tour.'

'Us in particular and no one else?' Grace asked, puzzled.

'I know, I think she's crazy too,' Jack said, grinning at them, 'but for some reason she wants you lot, and only you lot. She's waiting now.'

The girls made their way out to the reception and stopped short. There stood Mia, looking around her nervously. Even in her jeans and coat, it was obvious she was a dancer. She was so slender and yet you could tell she was strong and supple too.

'Hi again,' she said shyly. 'I was hoping you could show me around.'

'Sure, come this way,' Hannah said, leading Mia towards the first door, which was the drawing room.

'Daniel and Josh are doing some stuff with the soundtrack in that room,' Jack said. 'You should probably leave it till last.'

'Oh right,' Hannah said. 'Well then, how about the ballroom first? It's just down this corridor over here.'

Mia followed the four friends down the corridor and through the double doors into the ballroom. Inside, she stood looking around, wide-eyed.

'Wow, I didn't know this place even had a ballroom,' she said. 'It's fantastic. And look at that floor!' She began doing some little jumps on the wooden boards. 'It's just made for dancing.'

The girls watched her as she tested the floor, lost in her own world, a delighted smile on her face.

'I came up to talk to you, of course,' she said over her shoulder, 'but now I think I will get you to give me a full tour. It's really interesting, isn't it?'

Sarah smiled at her. 'It does get under your skin pretty quickly,' she agreed. 'We'll definitely give you the full tour.'

'First, though,' Abi said, 'what did you want to talk to us about?'

The girls looked eagerly at Mia, waiting to hear what she had to say. She stopped jumping about and came over to them.

'I said I'd think about your crazy story, and I did,' she said. 'It's still crazy to me, but I can't help thinking about Felicity and that her life wasn't very happy, and it seems so unfair that her afterlife should be unhappy too. So I don't know what it is I can do to help, but if there's anything, I'm here to do it.' She smiled at them nervously. 'I thought, if Felicity was here –' Mia looked around as if she expected some ghostly demon to pop out of the walls – 'she could see me again and maybe that would help her, if that's what she wants?'

'That is so good of you,' Abi said, touching Mia's arm gently. 'I know the thought of it must be scary. It's awesome that you're willing to do that.'

'Let's just do it quickly before I change my mind,' Mia said with an anxious laugh.

'All right,' Sarah said with a nod. She looked around the room and called out, 'Felicity,' as loudly as she dared. She didn't want to bring any of the other volunteers running. 'Grace,' she said, 'would you stand at the door and keep lookout – we don't want anyone to barge in here.' Grace scooted off to the double doors to stand guard.

'Felicity, I need to talk to you!' Sarah called out.

The air began to shimmer in the centre of the ballroom and suddenly Felicity was there.

'Hi,' Sarah said, smiling at her. 'Thanks for coming.'

Felicity was staring at Mia, obviously shocked to see her there. Mia was standing beside Abi and Hannah, looking around fearfully, not at all sure what would happen next. She noticed the four girls all looking at the same spot in the middle of the room and her body tensed up.

'Is she here now?' she asked Abi and Hannah in a whisper.

'Yes,' Abi said, nodding.

'Hi, Felicity,' Mia whispered. 'I hope it's OK that I'm here.'

Sarah raised her eyebrow at Felicity, and Felicity

nodded slowly. 'Tell her it's nice to see her,' Felicity said, sounding very different from the over-confident young girl they had first met.

Sarah turned to Mia. 'She says it's nice to see you.'

Mia nodded and swallowed hard. Abi put her hand on her arm to reassure her. Sarah was about to talk to Felicity again, when Mia surprised her by speaking up.

'Felicity,' Mia said, her voice a bit stronger now, 'I don't really know if these girls are telling the truth, so I'm going to ask you a question – something they can't know about. If you can answer it, I'll know you're really here.'

Felicity nodded at Sarah, and Sarah nodded at Mia. 'Go on,' she said.

Mia cleared her throat. 'When we performed a scene together at the gala night in your school, what mistake did I make?'

Felicity smirked at the memory. 'Tell her that she didn't keep her foot in front of her knee when she did a pirouette and was slightly unbalanced when she finished.'

Sarah repeated Felicity's answer word for word. Mia took a long, slow breath. 'OK, she's really here.' She looked at the four girls and it was plain to see the admiration in her eyes. 'For a bunch of kids, you're pretty amazing, you know that?' she said. 'This is some secret to keep.'

'But you will keep it, won't you?' Abi asked anxiously.

Mia nodded. 'It stays here in this room,' she replied. 'I won't tell a soul.' She turned to face the centre of the room, even though she couldn't see Felicity. She looked where the girls seemed to be looking. 'Felicity, I'm so sorry that you're not at peace and I'm so sorry about your accident. Everyone was really shocked and sad.'

Felicity looked down at the floor. 'Thanks, Mia. I wish things were different too.'

Sarah gulped down the lump forming in her throat and relayed this to Mia.

'What can we do to help you?' Mia asked.

'I'm not really sure,' Felicity replied.

'She says she's not really sure,' Sarah said, 'but we've had an idea.'

Felicity and Mia both looked at her with interest.

'Well, Felicity wants to perform the role she never got to dance,' Sarah explained, 'so how would you both feel about doing that dance together? We're not sure exactly how to do it, but if Felicity can dance *Snow White*, then maybe she can let go of the past and move on.' There was silence. 'What do you think, Felicity, Mia?' Sarah asked hopefully.

Felicity nodded mutely, but she looked pre-occupied. She was staring at Mia and she looked like her mind wasn't really on what Sarah was saying. Suddenly, Mia's eyes widened and she began laughing breathlessly.

'I've got it!' she said. 'I've just had the best idea *ever.*'

'What is it?' Sarah demanded.

'This place,' Mia said, extending her arms to take in the ballroom. 'Why don't we stage it here? It's perfect.'

'What, now?' Sarah said, looking around her.

'Oh no, much better than that,' Mia said, smiling. 'We're rehearsing our Christmas performance at the moment – it's a mix of different scenes from different ballets. What if we held the show here? My mum has been dreaming of a decent performance space for years and I think this could be it. We could charge for tickets, and that would make money for the museum and the academy. We could build a stage up that end and the highlight of the night could be a performance of a scene from *Snow White*. We can hold it on the twenty-second, so it's exactly six years to the night since Felicity's accident. It will commemorate her life and her dancing. I can rehearse between now and then – and I'll insist that I dance it alone, with everyone to imagine Felicity dancing with me. Only you four will be able to see what's really happening, but it will be amazing.' Mia stopped to draw breath. She was trembling with excitement at the idea of the performance, and it was infectious.

'Please let me do the decorating of the room,' Grace said from her post at the door. 'I could do a Christmas theme – whites and reds – it will be gorgeous.'

They were all caught up in the images they were conjuring up in their minds, when Sarah remembered Felicity, still standing there quietly. She turned to her. 'Are you OK with this, Felicity?' she asked.

The ballerina nodded at her and attempted a smile. 'It sounds so good,' she said. 'I love it.'

Mia noticed Sarah talking quietly to the empty space in front of her. 'Is this what Felicity wants?' she asked.

'Yes, she says she loves the idea,' Sarah replied.

'I'm so pleased,' Mia said. 'Felicity, is the scene where the Witch gives Snow White the apple a good one to do?'

'That's a good choice,' Felicity said, nodding. 'If Lauren is still at the academy, she could do the Witch to Mia's Snow White.'

'She says yes and that Lauren could dance the Witch's part with you,' Sarah said.

Mia shook her head firmly. 'No, I won't have anyone dance with me.'

'Tell her it won't work otherwise,' Felicity insisted.

'She says it won't work like that,' Sarah told Mia.

'It will,' Mia said. She tried to follow Sarah's gaze again and pick the spot where Felicity was standing. 'Felicity, you were the best Snow White we've ever had. I'll dance the Witch, you dance Snow White. I know the audience will only see one dancer on stage, but I'll give it my all and they can picture the rest. I think it will be more beautiful and more poignant to have your . . . absence on the stage. It's the right way to do it. I'll know that you're dancing with me, that's all that matters.'

Felicity bent her head and Sarah was astounded to see her little body shake with tears. She didn't know what to say. Abi whispered to Mia, 'She's crying, but I think it might be in a good way.'

'Actually,' Mia said suddenly, 'there's something else that might work. I don't know how Felicity would feel about this, but my mum recorded some of the rehearsals – remember, Felicity? She used it to show us our mistakes. I wonder if we could have a television or something on stage and show the footage of Felicity dancing?'

'Wow, that would be some performance,' Grace said, bowled over by the notion.

'I'll look into it,' Mia said. Sarah could tell from her face that her mind was whirling with ideas and plans.

'It means we've a huge amount to do between now and the twenty-second, though,' Hannah reminded them. 'It's only a week away. I'm not sure it's possible.'

'Well, we'll certainly be ready,' Mia said. 'We've been rehearsing for the last six weeks. So once you can get this place ready for us, then there's no problem. We've a ready-made audience with all the parents of the ballet kids. We can just tell them there's a venue change, then sell tickets at the door. If it's for the good of the academy and the museum, I can't see anyone complaining.'

Hannah nodded. 'OK then, we'll talk to Miss Flood and the volunteers right now.'

'Quick,' Grace called suddenly from the doors, 'someone's coming.'

They raced to the centre of the room – feeling like they had to shield Felicity, which was silly given that no one else could see her. Mia stood with them, trying to look like an interested visitor and Hannah launched into a loud description of the ballroom. The door pushed open and a head popped round the frame.

Simone.

'Oh, it's only you,' Grace said with relief. 'Come in.'

'Hi, Grace,' Simone said, sounding unsure of herself. 'Look, I know you're probably angry at me. I feel bad about the other day. So I just wanted to –' She stopped abruptly. Simone stared at Mia. She looked like she might turn and run at any moment. Mia took a step forward. Sarah could see a blush rise up Simone's face. She'd never seen her look like that before – she looked so . . . shame-faced.

'Hi, Simone,' Mia said quickly. 'The girls told me everything. Felicity is here now.'

Simone's eyes registered fear and she gasped. 'What?' she said faintly. 'Why?'

'No, it's good,' Mia said, dismayed by how shaken Simone looked. 'She needs our help and we think we've figured out what to do.'

Sarah looked at Felicity. She was staring hard at Simone and looked almost as stricken. Sarah felt a strange shivery sensation across her skin. It wasn't nice. Sarah looked from Felicity, to Mia, to Simone and suddenly she felt angry with all three of them. 'All right,' she said firmly, the frustration clear in her voice, 'what is it with you three? There is definitely something you're not telling us and I want to know what it is.'

Six faces turned to look at her with startled expressions.

'I've had it,' Sarah said angrily, 'you're hiding something. Out with it.'

Simone looked like a caged animal. Her face was red and her breathing was coming in quick gasps. 'I'm sorry,' she said, her voice breaking. 'I'm so sorry . . .' With that, she turned and marched back down the corridor. Grace took off after her, but returned a few moments later.

'She left,' she said simply, but she looked upset. Simone's behaviour had been so out of character for ages now.

'Don't worry, it's me, not you,' Mia said. 'She doesn't want to be around me.' She looked very upset. She walked back to her bag and picked it up. 'I'd better go. I'll talk to my mum about the performance idea when I get home. You can text me later to let me know if your teacher agreed to everything.' She turned back to the centre of the room and wiped a tear from her eye. 'Tell Felicity I'll do my best.' Then she too turned quickly on her heel and marched out.

'Oh no,' Sarah said suddenly, as she saw the air near her begin to shimmer. 'Wait, Felicity, don't –'

It was too late. Felicity had disappeared as well.

Sarah, Abi, Hannah and Grace stood looking at each other. The sudden silence in the ballroom was unnerving.

'What *actually* happened in that dance school?' Sarah said, voicing what they were all thinking.

'Curiouser and curiouser,' Hannah whispered, almost to herself.

13

Plans and Preparations

There was very little time to plan a whole evening event at the museum, so the girls were forced to put all thoughts of Simone, Mia and Felicity out of their minds for the time being and focus on the show. They rushed off to find Miss Flood. She was in the garden, of course, but she listened to their breathless description of ballet performances and fund-raising for the museum.

'OK, OK, slow down, girls,' she said, holding up her gloved hand. 'I'm catching some of what you're saying, but not all. You think we can hold a performance in one week's time?' She looked far from convinced.

'Just hear us out, Miss,' Grace pleaded. 'We really think we can make it work.'

Miss Flood stuck her spade upright in the ground and removed her heavy duty gloves. 'All right, let's go inside and gather the others. We'll have to take this decision together.'

The word went round that a volunteers' meeting

would be held in the sitting room just after closing. At four o'clock Jack closed and locked the front door, and they all filtered into the room, throwing themselves into stuffed armchairs and on to long couches. Abi, Hannah, Sarah and Grace sat together at the top of the room next to Miss Flood. Chrissy's eyes narrowed when she saw them taking charge of things, and she and Elaine started whispering to each other.

'The girls here,' Miss Flood began, indicating the friends, 'have an idea to put to us. We're going to listen to it in full, then decide together if we want to do it.'

She sat down, and Hannah stood up, looking nervous.

'Is this another fascinating discovery, like the Henry Grainger thing?' Chrissy demanded in a bored voice.

'No, it's very different,' Hannah said without even bothering to look at her. 'It's about ballet.'

Chrissy looked surprised at that, and she went quiet.

'What we're going to suggest will sound impossible at first,' Hannah said, 'but it would be wonderful if we could pull it off.' She explained how one of the visitors that day had been Mia Roseman of the Roseman Academy, and how she had fallen in love with the ballroom and suggested a joint production. 'It has to take place on the twenty-second, though,'

Hannah admitted, 'which means just one week to sort it all out.'

The volunteers looked at each other and Sarah could see that they thought it couldn't be done. She crossed her fingers, hoping they would agree to it.

'I know that's a lot of work,' Hannah continued, 'but some things are already done – like the academy has over fifty people booked to come along. Mia's idea was that we could charge at the door, then split the money between here and the academy.'

'But why does it have to be next week?' Daniel asked. 'Can't we just do it in the New Year instead?'

'No, it has to be that particular night,' Hannah insisted. 'There was a ballet student who died six years ago.'

Daniel looked around at the other volunteers and they all looked confused. 'What does that have to do with this?' he asked Hannah.

'Well, she died on the night of their Christmas performance – on the twenty-second of December 2006. She should have been in the starring role that night, but she was knocked down by a car on the way to the dance and she died. Mia wants to perform that dance now to mark the anniversary of Felicity's death.'

Hannah paused, and Sarah reckoned a pin dropping would have sounded like an avalanche – the volunteers were staring at Hannah, trying to take in what she was saying. Suddenly they had gone from ballet dancing to fatal accidents – it was hard to keep up.

'I didn't realize there was a story like that behind this idea,' Miss Flood remarked. 'How you lot ferret out these things I really don't know.'

'Well, that's the suggestion,' Hannah said, 'and we're really, really hoping you'll all agree to do this. It would be a great night.' She sat down again and looked at her friends: had they done enough to convince the rest?

'Right then, let's put it to a vote,' Miss Flood said. 'Anyone in favour of the ballet show, raise your hand.'

To the girls' surprise, Chrissy and Elaine's hands shot up into the air. No one else moved. Daniel, Solomon, Jack and Josh all looked at the floor, and their hands stayed put.

'Why are you in favour, Chrissy?' Miss Flood asked. Sarah smiled to herself – obviously even Miss Flood was curious to know why Chrissy was actually supporting something.

'My friend Sophie is an amazing dancer,' Chrissy gushed, 'and she has a big part in one of the scenes, so I'd like to see her dance here and steal the show.' Her swaggering confidence made Sarah want to laugh out loud, but she kept her lips closed tightly.

'OK,' Miss Flood said, nodding. 'Now, all four boys disagree, am I right?'

The boys nodded.

'Why's that?' Miss Flood asked.

It was Josh who spoke up. 'I don't like shooting down another volunteer's suggestion,' he said, glancing up at the four girls, 'but I think it's too much for one week. I don't know anything about ballet, but I know a performance needs a stage and all sorts of things to make it work – we just don't have the time to do it.'

Solomon, Jack and Daniel all murmured their agreement, and Miss Flood looked around the room at the ten children. She looked uncertain as to what to do next.

'This is a bit awkward,' she said finally. 'The four girls have presented the proposition together, so I don't know whether to take their votes separately or as one. Obviously if we add in their four votes, the boys are immediately outvoted. My own vote would be no, I'd have to say. I think Josh is right about the amount of work. That would make it six to five in favour, but that's a very slim margin.'

Hannah was about to make another point to try to sway them, when suddenly there was a thunderous banging on the front door.

'Someone *really* wants to visit the museum,' Sarah remarked. 'That person is seriously eager to get in here.'

'I'll check it out,' Miss Flood said, smiling at Sarah, and she left the room.

While she was gone, Josh looked over at the four

friends. 'Hey, I'm sorry we're not behind this,' he said. 'I'd be happy to do it in a month, but a week is just too short.'

'Don't worry, Josh,' Hannah reassured him, 'you have to speak your mind when you have an opinion. That's fine.'

'Aw, do you want Abi to kiss it better, Joshie?' Chrissy said in a simpering voice, making Elaine cackle with laughter.

Abi blushed bright red and stared at her shoes. Josh ignored the remark, but Sarah couldn't help herself. 'Shut it, Chrissy,' she warned.

The door to the sitting room suddenly slammed open, making them all jump. A tall, thin woman dressed all in black strode into the room, energy and briskness fairly crackling off her.

'Where are Abi, Hannah, Grace and Sarah?' demanded Marcella Roseman.

Sarah gulped. What had gone wrong now?

The four girls meekly raised their hands and Marcella Roseman swung round to face them. Suddenly, her face broke into a stiff smile. 'Well, I had written you lot off as odd little girls,' she said in what was meant to be a warm voice, 'but you've impressed me now.'

The girls were astounded – was Marcella Roseman actually telling them she was pleased with them?

'Miss Flood,' she said, turning to face their

dumbstruck teacher, 'this proposal to use the ballroom for our performance is absolutely wonderful. We are delighted with it and want to get going straight away. Now, let's go see the ballroom and figure out what we have to do.'

She strode out of the room, oblivious to the shocked silence she left in her wake. Miss Flood and her ten volunteers looked at each other. From outside in the reception area the human tornado that was Marcella Roseman barked at them, 'Come on, lots to do, very little time!'

Miss Flood looked towards the doorway, then back at the children. 'I suppose we'd better follow her,' she said finally. 'I'm really not sure what's going on now.'

'It looks like we're staging a ballet show next week,' Josh said drily, 'whether we like it or not.'

They all filed outside and straggled down the corridor after the ballet teacher. The girls went ahead and showed her to the ballroom. When they pulled open the double doors and stepped inside, Marcella breathed a sigh of delight.

'It's perfect,' she said, clasping her hands together. 'Just perfect.'

'Well, it's not really,' Miss Flood interrupted. 'There's no stage, for starters. It's really not ready for –'

'You are forgetting the resources I have at my disposal,' Marcella replied dismissively. 'I have a stage crew who do the whole set-up and design. I'll have them over here on Monday. We'll set up the stage down there,' she said, pointing to the far end of the room, 'then the chairs will fill this part, and we can make it look as nice as we can in the time allowed.'

'But –' Miss Flood tried again. She was cut off quickly.

'You can have the desk outside working as a ticket office, that's easy,' went on Marcella, 'and I'll get the dancers in for a dress rehearsal on Wednesday. We'll split the proceeds fifty–fifty, that's only fair. And the children here can dig in and help us out too.'

Sarah looked at Miss Flood and giggled. She'd never seen her teacher caught off guard before, but she looked like her head was spinning at the force of Marcella Roseman's determination. It seemed like the ballet performance was definitely going ahead now!

Grace raised her hand timidly.

'Yes?' Marcella barked at her.

'I'd like to be involved in the decorating of the room,' Grace said. 'I'm really into that sort of thing, and I'd love to do a Christmas theme with –'

'Fantastic,' Marcella interrupted her. 'You're in charge of room decoration then. Come up to the academy between now and Tuesday. We have a room full of props and fabrics and all sorts of odds and ends. You'll find what you need there.'

Grace looked like she had just received a personal invitation to Aladdin's cave. She grinned widely and looked thoroughly delighted with herself.

'Finally,' Marcella went on, 'I think we should also add another element to the night – namely, have a supper dance after the performance.'

'A . . . supper dance?' Miss Flood said faintly. 'Really?'

'Absolutely, Miss Flood. That means everyone gets dressed up, there's a great sense of occasion and Christmas festivity, and we can charge more on the ticket. I'll organize a buffet supper with my sister – she runs the Riverside Restaurant, you know. It won't be a problem. We'll just move the chairs out of the way after the performance, then let everyone back into the ballroom for some music. They'll love it, guaranteed.'

All the girls present, including Chrissy and Elaine, looked thrilled at this suggestion. That meant they had to dress up, which would be much more fun than wearing their usual uniform of T-shirt and trousers.

'Right then,' Marcella Roseman said briskly. 'That's all decided.'

She looked at them for confirmation, and no one disagreed with her.

'I'm thrilled to be working with you all,' she went on. 'We'll have great fun making this happen.' She strode towards the double doors, but then turned back as she reached them. 'And take those bewildered looks off your faces,' she ordered, 'a week is plenty of time!'

14

Big Bully

'I've changed my mind about this,' Jack announced. 'I think this ballet thing is a brilliant idea altogether.'

It was Wednesday morning, and the volunteers had just arrived at the museum, ready for a day's work.

'Would that change of heart have anything to do with Miss Flood getting us off school early?' Grace asked.

'No, not at all,' Jack protested. His face broke into a grin to show he was joking. Grace burst out laughing. 'Are you kidding me?' Jack went on. 'You four have just given me the best Christmas present ever – time off school!'

Miss Flood had gone to the principal to explain about the big event at the museum that Saturday night, and she had agreed that the volunteers could finish on Tuesday, rather than at lunchtime on Thursday like the rest of the school. So here they were in their oldest jeans and jumpers, ready to work on getting things ready for the show.

Inside, the museum felt completely different from usual – there was a hum of work in progress, people shouting out to each other, the sound of a drill gnawing away in the ballroom, and about twenty ballet students in rehearsal outfits, turning *pliés* and leaping about in the reception area, waiting for the rehearsal proper to begin. For the volunteers, it was the first time it didn't feel like 'their' museum and they stood uncertainly in the reception area, trying to keep out of the way until someone told them what exactly they should be doing.

The front door was standing open in spite of the icy wind to allow all the comings and goings to go on unimpeded. A man stepped through and looked around, then removed his glasses to clean them on his scarf.

'Mr Roseman,' Grace called out excitedly. 'Hello again.' She ran over to him and he smiled broadly at her.

'Hello, Grace, good to see you. I've brought all the boxes you stacked up – the car is packed to the rafters. Can you give me a hand?'

'Of course,' Grace said, then she turned to the volunteers. 'Can you help me unload the car?'

They went outside and started pulling out box after box from Mr Roseman's car. There were about fifteen boxes in all.

'What is all this, Grace?' Daniel asked as he

hefted a heavy box across the reception area that Sarah had had trouble lifting.

'Treasures,' Grace said, her eyes sparkling with anticipation at the thought of getting stuck into the decorating. 'I found some incredible stuff up at the academy. I cannot wait to get into the ballroom and get going. I've got some great ideas.'

Sarah, Hannah and Abi smiled at each other – that heart-warming enthusiasm was why they loved their friend so much.

There came the sound of a sharp clap and they looked up to see Marcella Roseman standing in the corridor in front of the doors to the ballroom.

'All right, everyone,' she called out, 'come on in and have a look.'

The dancers, the volunteers, the straggling workmen and Mr Roseman all filed down the corridor and into the ballroom. Sarah's eyes were wide as she took in the transformation.

At the end of the long room, the carpenters had built a wooden stage, using a protective rubber base to protect the floor underneath it. It spanned almost the width of the room and looked very impressive. The stage designer had also been hard at work, and there were beautifully decorated Christmas trees on either side of the stage, a cleverly painted fabric backdrop and black dividing curtain walls so the audience couldn't see into the wings. They had brought the stage curtains from the auditorium at the academy – two heavy red velvet curtains operated by a makeshift pulley system. On the right-hand side of the stage, a long screen had been unfurled from the overhead light rigging.

The assembled crowd looked at everything, then burst into applause. The workmen grinned at each other and took a bow, making everyone laugh. They had fit about four days' work into two days, and looked pleased to be finished.

'Now then,' Marcella called out above the rush of voices, 'I want all the dancers round the stage area, please. We'll rehearse the scenes in sequence, starting with Sophie as the Sugar Plum Fairy. Come on. Quickly, quickly.'

The workmen started to pack their things and leave. Grace went up to them to ask if they could leave behind a ladder so she could decorate the walls.

'I've a feeling she's going to be keeping us very busy,' Abi said to Hannah and Sarah with a smile, watching Grace buzz about the room, sizing up the space.

Sarah looked around happily at all the activity and noise. 'I don't mind at all,' she said. Abi and Hannah looked at her in surprise. 'You don't?' asked Hannah.

'No, I think it's great to have all this going on. I mean, what else would we be doing but sitting at home worrying about Christmas? This is great.'

Abi and Hannah exchanged a look.

'Are you talking about Christmas without your dad?' Hannah said gently.

Sarah looked at them and nodded quickly. 'I suppose so,' she said. 'He's going to come over for dinner, but it's just going to be weird, you know, to not have him there as usual.' She pushed her hair behind her ears and focused on not letting her eyes well up with tears as they were threatening to do.

'That's really hard,' Abi said softly. 'You know, my mom is crazy about Christmas and loves having people over, so if ever you want a break from your place, or need some company, come straight over to us. Honestly, any time.'

Sarah smiled at her. 'Thanks so much, Abi,' she said, squeezing her friend's hand. 'I will definitely do that if it all gets too much.'

'Guys, you won't believe it,' Grace cried as she ran over to join them. 'I just asked the stage designer about the screen, and they *do* have footage of Felicity dancing. That's what the screen is for – they're going to use the projector to put up the rehearsal film so she'll kind of be dancing with Mia.'

'Crikey,' Hannah said, 'that's amazing. In fact, it'll probably be a little strange to watch it – sort of ghostly in its own way.'

'I know,' Grace said, nearly shaking with

excitement. 'This is going to be incredible from start to finish!'

'Calm down, Grace,' Abi said, laughing, 'there's a whole three days to go until Saturday.'

'May I come in?' called a voice from the double doors.

The girls looked over and saw Mr Grainger smiling at them, and looking in wonder at the 'new' ballroom. He came over to them and whistled.

'Isn't this some sight?' he said. 'It's wonderful to see the old place come to life like this.'

'Will you be coming to the show?' Abi asked him.

'Oh, I wouldn't miss it for the world,' he replied. 'When you lot do an event it tends to be a memorable night.'

The girls smiled at each other – he had no idea just how memorable it was going to be!

He turned to them and his smile looked a little strained. 'I was hoping to catch the four of you actually,' he said quietly. 'Wanted to have a word, if that's OK?'

'Of course,' Hannah said immediately, 'what's up?'

Mr Grainger looked down at his gloves, then back at the girls. 'It's just that Simone seems out of sorts. I was wondering if perhaps you had had a falling out. Something like that, perhaps? I don't want to pry,' he said, looking embarrassed, 'but

I'm just a little worried about her and hoped she hadn't lost her new friends.'

'We're still here,' Sarah said, 'but she has been acting strangely lately. We don't know why, though. It just seems something is bothering her, but she won't talk to us about it.'

'I see,' Mr Grainger said, concern plain on his face. 'Thanks for being so honest,' he said to Sarah. 'I'll try to talk to her again, see if she's ready to open up.'

'We really want her back as our friend too,' Abi said. 'We miss her.'

Mr Grainger smiled. 'I hope that happens soon,' he said. 'She really enjoys having you lot to talk to.'

'Do you think she'll come with you on Saturday?' Grace asked. 'It would be really great if she was here for it.'

'I'll do my very best,' Mr Grainger promised. He turned his attention back to the ballroom. 'It's all very professional looking. Will you be ready in time?'

'I think so,' Grace said, looking around at the chaos. 'I'm getting going on the room decoration now, and the stage is done and the dancers are ready. I think most things are working.'

'Marvellous,' Mr Grainger said, smiling at everything.

'There is one problem, though,' Grace said,

frowning suddenly. 'I don't know how we're going to do things without a backstage area. It means the dancers have to come in the door up there, so the audience will see them coming in and climbing into the wings. It's not ideal.'

'Oh, I see,' Mr Grainger replied, looking at the set-up round the stage area. 'Well, Grace, it just so happens I have the perfect solution.'

'You do?' Grace said, surprised. 'What is it?'

'A hidden corridor,' Mr Grainger announced. 'Come on, I'll show you.'

They followed him up to the stage and then behind it. The workmen had built the stage away from the wall, leaving a gap of about two metres. Into this area behind the backdrop they slipped, and then over to the side wall. Mr Grainger looked up and down the wall for a moment, then leant forward and pressed a section of the wallpaper. The girls gasped – it was just like the writing-room door. The mechanism was invisible, but when he pressed the correct spot, a door suddenly sprang open quietly, revealing a narrow passageway.

'Where does it go to?' Grace asked, peering inside.

'To an ante-room that is located between here and the sitting room,' Mr Grainger replied. 'Clever, isn't it?'

'It sure is,' Grace said, smiling at him. 'It's exactly what we need. The dancers can prepare in the ante-room and join the stage this way, without anyone seeing them.'

'Glad I could be of service,' Mr Grainger said. 'Now, I'd better get out of the way and leave you all to your work. See you on Saturday.' He wandered off, stepping over toolboxes and round dancers.

The four friends looked at each other in delight.

'Let's go tell Marcella about the hidden backstage area,' Sarah said with a grin. 'This is going to blow her mind!'

By lunchtime, the volunteers were famished. They had worked with focus all morning and it was time for a break. The dancers didn't seem to need breaks, so they left the ballroom to them and the ten volunteers made their way to the kitchen to have their sandwiches there.

They sat on stools round the butcher's-block table, although Chrissy and Elaine sat a little apart, perched on stools against the counter that ran along the wall either side of the cavernous fireplace.

'I'm beginning to think school would be far easier than this,' Solomon said wearily as he unwrapped his lunch. 'They're probably all messing about and doing no work in class at all.'

'Ah, this is still more fun,' Daniel said.

'Plus we're surrounded by dancers in tutus,' Jack added, 'which is quite interesting, I have to say.'

The other boys grinned at him, while the girls rolled their eyes.

There was a clatter of footsteps down the back stairs and Miss Flood joined them.

'Oh, you're all in here,' she said. 'I was just going to make myself a coffee. How are you all doing?'

'Fine, Miss,' they murmured.

'Miss Flood,' Chrissy said, 'I'd like to ask you something, please.'

Uh-oh, Sarah thought, *she's being super polite – not a good sign.*

'Yes, Chrissy,' their teacher said as she spooned coffee into her mug.

'Well, you know Sophie is one of the star performers on Saturday,' Chrissy began, 'and Elaine and myself are obviously on the museum team. I was hoping you could let Tiffany join us as a volunteer, so we're all involved in the event. We'd all like to be in it together, you know, as friends.'

Miss Flood kept her back to them all while she poured water into the mug and stirred the coffee. Then she turned round to face Chrissy.

'I do understand that,' she said, 'but I really can't go back to the principal and ask for another student to be given time off. We do have enough people, Chrissy – ten is perfect. I hope you aren't too disappointed.'

A silence had descended on the group as they

watched Chrissy for her reaction. She was struggling to keep her sweet smile plastered on her face, but her eyes had that dangerous glint they had all come to know. Miss Flood was being as nice as possible, but it was clear that wasn't the answer Chrissy wanted to hear.

'I really don't think it's fair, Miss,' she tried again, 'to keep someone out who wants to be part of the volunteer team. Tiffany's been waiting since September to get her chance.'

'Chrissy,' Miss Flood said quietly, 'I invited people to sign up for this and you ten got lucky. I have lots of kids wanting to be involved now that it's a success and I can't accommodate everyone. You'll just have to be thankful you put your name down quickly and enjoy it for yourself, OK?'

Nine heads swivelled back to Chrissy, who flicked her black curls and squared her shoulders.

'Miss, I really didn't want to have to say this,' she began, 'but two of the volunteers have been acting . . . inappropriately. I think you should know that. It's not fair that they should be here and others don't get a chance.'

Beside her, Sarah felt Abi's body stiffen. She glanced at her friend and could see her fists clenched on the table. The whole atmosphere in the room had changed now and felt like it could explode at any moment.

'Abi,' Chrissy said, turning on her stool to look

over at her, 'you really should do the decent thing and give up your place right now.'

Abi bit her lip. 'No, I will not, Chrissy,' she said in a strangled voice, 'and you know full well that there is no reason for me to do that.'

'Oh, no reason, really?' Chrissy said, getting into her stride. 'You don't think carrying on with Josh is a reason, then? I think it's pretty bad behaviour for a girl your age.'

Abi stared Chrissy down, but Sarah wondered how long she could keep herself in check. Sarah knew she'd end up bursting into angry tears if she was in Abi's shoes right now.

'That is not true,' Abi said through gritted teeth.

'Well that photograph that turned up on the noticeboard in school seemed to tell a different story.'

'Chrissy,' Miss Flood said firmly, 'I want you to stop this now. You can't bully your way into getting what you want. Not with me. I don't want to hear any of your nasty gossip any more and I don't want it repeated anywhere else either. Do you understand me?'

'Look at her,' Chrissy shouted, pointing at Abi. 'She's obviously lying – her face is red and she –'

Without warning, Chrissy's rant was interrupted by a clatter of brass as one of the large cooking pots hanging on the rack above her head dislodged itself and crashed down on her, glancing off her shoulder before hitting the floor with a ringing crash.

No one moved. No one spoke. Everyone was staring at the pot on the floor. Slowly, they looked up at Chrissy. Her face was white, and she was holding her shoulder with one hand.

'Are you all right, Chrissy?' Miss Flood asked. Chrissy nodded slowly like someone waking up from a dream.

'That was freaky,' Elaine whispered. 'Those things have never fallen down before. How did that happen?'

Sarah looked towards the rack and her mouth fell open: the air was shimmering violently round it. *Felicity!*

'Pick up that pot, Elaine,' Miss Flood said. 'That's the end of that. Chrissy, don't bring up this subject again.' She took her coffee and went back up the stairs, leaving the volunteers looking around in shock.

Elaine put the pot on the counter, then went to put her arm protectively round her friend. 'Come on,' she said, walking her towards the stairs. 'You were only trying to do the right thing, but they just don't see that.'

Josh scraped back his chair loudly and went quickly up the stairs, not saying a word to anyone. Sarah hoped he wasn't going to throttle Chrissy – he looked so angry. Daniel, Jack and Solomon quietly followed after him, with a few backward glances at Abi, who was still sitting with her fists clenched on the table.

When everyone had left, the girls leant in to Abi and hugged her. They didn't know what to say. Grace went over to the pot and climbed on the stool in order to hang it back in its rightful place. As she did so, a chill descended on the kitchen, then Felicity appeared. She looked upset.

'Way to go, Felicity,' Sarah said with a grin. 'Talk about taking a pot shot at Chrissy!'

The ghost didn't smile. She looked upset. 'I shouldn't have done that,' she whispered.

'Are you OK?' Grace asked. 'Don't worry about losing your temper. Chrissy was being so horrible to Abi, she deserved what she got.'

'She's just such a big bully,' Felicity wailed, then she burst into tears.

'Oh now, it's all right,' Abi said, jumping down from her stool and forgetting her own feelings in the face of Felicity's distress. 'Hey, don't be upset. You were just standing up for me.'

'You don't understand,' Felicity cried. Her little shoulders heaved with sobs and the whole room became icebox cold. 'You don't understand.'

'Then tell us,' Hannah implored her.

Sarah wished she could put her arms round the little girl – she looked so alone.

Felicity looked up at them and her eyes looked

fearful. 'I don't think I can.' She sniffed sadly. 'I'm just so . . . ashamed.'

'Of what?' Sarah asked, thinking that it was a strong word for a ten-year-old to use. 'What could you have done that would make you feel ashamed?'

They waited as Felicity struggled to compose herself and say the words that clearly frightened her. 'I was . . . I was a dreadful bully.'

'You?' Grace said, shocked. 'No way.'

Felicity nodded. 'I was. I bullied Mia all the time. I can't believe I was so awful to her. She had her mother driving her crazy too, and I made everything worse. I wish I had been different.'

The girls were taken aback by this confession. Sure, Felicity had been a bit rude the first time they met her, but a full-on bully? It just didn't seem to fit.

'Why did you do it?' Sarah asked simply.

'Mia was such a good dancer,' Felicity said in a flat voice. 'I was afraid she'd beat me. If she did, I knew my mother would be so angry. I was terrified of my mother and of failing.'

'It doesn't really sound like it was your fault,' Abi said gently.

Felicity looked at her with some of her old poutiness. 'Don't say stuff like that just because I'm young. You can't kid me, I *know* it was my fault. I had a choice and I chose to be nasty to her. It is my fault. When I saw that horrible Chrissy girl picking on you, I saw myself – and I hated it.'

Hannah was looking at the ghost intently. 'Felicity,' she said, 'do you think this could be why you're still here?'

The ghost and her friends all looked at her. 'What do you mean?' Felicity asked.

'I mean, that the reason you can't rest in peace is because you never got a chance to say sorry to Mia.'

Good old Hannah, thought Sarah, *right on the button as usual*.

Felicity looked at Hannah in surprise – obviously the idea had never occurred to her before.

'I think if you say all this to Mia,' Hannah continued, 'you might find that a big weight is lifted from you.'

'I . . . I don't know,' Felicity said, looking frightened again. 'It's all so long ago now.'

'That doesn't mean it's stopped hurting,' Abi said.

'I just don't know if that's the answer,' Felicity said with a sigh. The air round her began to shimmer and she disappeared.

The four friends were left alone.

'You're right, Hannah,' Sarah said. 'I bet that's it.'

'It's hard to get your head round, isn't it?' Grace asked. 'And the fact that Mia has been so good about this. She mustn't hold a grudge at all.'

Hannah looked over at Abi. 'Are you OK?' she asked.

163

Abi nodded. 'I know Felicity was upset about it,' she said, 'but I am so glad she landed that pot on top of Chrissy. I just wish she'd had better aim!' The girls burst out laughing.

15

Getting Ready

It was Saturday at last, and all the work had paid off. The house was as ready as it would ever be, with the reception desk set up to serve as a ticket office. The museum and the academy had come together and worked flat out to make sure everything was perfect – and it was.

The ballroom was simply stunning. Grace had gone all out on her Christmas theme. There was a line of poinsettia plants in white pots along both walls. Grace had insisted they cover every single chair with white seat covers and red ribbons. Sarah grumbled with every bow she tied, but it had been worth it. Plain old plastic seats would have looked dull, but, now, it really looked like a ballroom – pretty and elegant. In the props room at the academy Grace had come across a big box of worn-out old dancing shoes, and in a moment of inspiration she had decided to spray them white and red. These shoes now hung along the walls at intervals, suspended from red ribbons and speaking of the memories of dances past. Grace had added red satin ribbons to the chandelier in the centre of the ceiling too. And she had used round shallow glass bowls from the academy as unusual light-holders, filling them with bunches of fairy lights and placing the bowls at different points around the room and stage. The whole effect was magical – it was like stepping back in time. Sarah kept thinking an old-style waltz would start up at any moment, and dancers would come out to sashay across the floor.

'Grace, Grace, Grace,' Marcella Roseman called out as she crossed over to where the girls were standing, admiring everything. 'You are gifted, my dear, absolutely gifted!'

Grace blushed, but she was thrilled that everyone loved what she'd done for the performance.

'Honestly, Grace,' Marcella went on, 'I want you to come work for me and design every show from now on. You have a great future ahead of you.'

Mia walked up behind her mother. 'Oh, you're making her blush, Mum,' she teased. 'But you have done an incredible job,' she added, smiling at Grace and the girls.

'I want to check the lights one last time,' Marcella said and she strode off towards the stage.

'She's so happy about this,' Mia said, looking after her mother. 'I'm delighted for her.'

'How about you?' Sarah asked. 'Are you ready for your big dance?'

Mia nodded. 'I'm really nervous about how it will work,' she admitted, 'but I've been practising hard and I'm ready. Do you think Felicity is ready too?'

The girls glanced at each other – they hadn't mentioned what had happened in the kitchen the other day and Felicity's confession about being a bully. They felt that was between Mia and Felicity.

'I think she's looking forward to it,' Abi replied.

'By the way, I brought the photograph today, Grace.'

'Thanks, Mia. I want to set it up outside, at the entrance to the corridor leading down here.'

'What photograph?' Sarah asked.

'I asked Marcella if I could borrow the big photo of Felicity that we saw hanging in the academy,' Grace told them. 'She agreed. Seeing as we're celebrating Felicity's life, I thought it would be nice to have a reminder of her for everyone.'

'That's an awesome idea,' Abi said, clapping Grace gently on the back.

Mia looked at her watch. 'Right, time to go home for some food and a nap. I guess I'll see you all here at show time.'

'Bye, Mia,' Grace said, 'and good luck.'

'And, please, *don't* break a leg,' Sarah joked.

'We should be getting going soon too,' Grace said. 'We have a lot of dressing up to do!'

'I wanted to show you all one thing,' Sarah said. 'Just an idea I had. It's outside in my bag.'

The other girls followed Sarah back to the reception area and she grabbed her bag from under the counter. 'Let's go up to the nursery,' she said quietly. They went up the curving staircase to the first floor, then into the nursery and closed the door.

'What is it?' Abi asked curiously.

From her bag, Sarah pulled out a stiff piece of card. She had made it herself and obviously taken a lot of time over it. It was an invitation, in black and gold lettering:

You are cordially invited to:

'*The Final Dance*'

a unique ballet performance
by Felicity Fenston and Mia Roseman

The two stars of the Roseman Academy will tonight perform together in a scene from Snow White.

This dance will celebrate the life of Felicity, who is sadly missed by all her friends.

It will be an unforgettable ballet experience!

'Wow!' Abi breathed. 'That looks fantastic, Sarah.'

'That is so lovely,' Hannah said, smiling at Sarah. 'I think she'll really love it.'

Sarah grinned. 'I thought I'd leave it here – you know, the first place we met her. Hopefully she'll see it and know that everything will be OK. I think I owe her this after being so "direct" with her.'

Hannah laughed. 'That's one word for it, Sarah.'

'You know,' said Grace, 'it's so good, I think we should blow it up on the photocopier and make a poster – it could hang next to the photo of Felicity.'

'Really?' Sarah said, pleased that Grace thought she had done such a good job. 'Well, that's OK by me if you think it'll work.'

'Definitely,' Grace announced. 'And now, ladies, it's time to finish up and go home to put on our party dresses.'

'Hear, hear,' Sarah said, rubbing her hands together. 'This is going to be so much fun!'

As planned, the four girls met in Abi's house to get ready for the ballet and supper dance. Grace's mother had put a lot of work into their dresses. They all wanted full-length dresses because they'd never worn them before, so Mrs Quinn had trawled through the rails of the local charity shops to find four dresses she could alter. When they walked into Abi's bedroom, the dresses were hung up on the wardrobe all in a line. They looked like paper-doll outfits, waiting to be filled.

'OK, some music to set the scene,' Abi said, flicking on the stereo. 'Now, don't laugh, you guys, but I'm going to let you into the secret of my favourite music.' The sound of the Jackson Five filled the room, and Sarah, Hannah and Grace immediately burst out laughing.

Hannah shook her head in mock despair. 'My mother listens to this stuff,' she teased Abi.

'Who knew you were an old time girl?' Sarah added. 'Although I have to admit, it does get the feet tapping.'

The girls started dancing wildly, throwing disco shapes all around the room until they were breathless. They fell on to Abi's bed, laughing at their own silliness.

'Hair time,' Grace called out. 'Who's doing what?'

They each decided whether to wear their hair up or down, then Grace set about plaiting and tying up and putting in curlers. When Abi's mother walked in with a tray of juice and cookies they looked a sight – wrapped in bath robes, hair in various stages of readiness, and cucumber slices held to their eyes for the 'sparkle effect', as Abi called it. Her mother started giggling when she saw them.

'I know we're not fit for public viewing yet,' Sarah said from under her cucumbers, 'but we'll be just gorgeous once we're done.'

'I'll have to take your word for that,' Abi's mother joked as she left.

After refuelling on the snacks, it was time to finish the process.

'All right, girls,' Abi said with a grin, 'time to get the dresses on!'

They took them down off the hangers very carefully and slid themselves inside, helping each other with buttons and zips. Then they stood back to admire one another. The dresses were beautiful – Grace's mother had picked simple designs in pretty colours, then nipped and tucked them to fit the girls perfectly. Hannah's dress was sea-blue, which went beautifully with her blonde hair. Sarah was wearing a cream-coloured dress with lace round the neck, which looked striking against her long red hair. Abi was in mint green, which set off her short brown hair and hazel eyes. Grace looked a picture: she had opted for a plain black dress, but then embellished it with a red sash, red elbow-high gloves and a big white feather in her hair. She looked like a glamorous actress in a black-and-white film.

The four of them swished about the room, twirling round and thoroughly enjoying looking completely different.

'So what do you think?' Grace said, doing a twirl, 'will we have the boys lining up to dance with us?'

Abi, Hannah and Sarah burst out laughing, although Sarah could see Abi blushing and she could feel the heat rise to her own cheeks too. She hadn't let herself think about the dancing part of things and she wouldn't have admitted it to anyone, but she secretly hoped Daniel might dance with her.

Abi's mother popped her head round the door again. 'Oh my goodness, you do look gorgeous,' she said, smiling at their transformation. 'Are you ready now, because your chariot awaits?'

'Thanks for the ride, Mom,' Abi said. 'I think we're ready.'

The girls smiled excitedly at each other – they were ready for whatever the night would bring.

16

A Grand Entrance

At the museum, a sense of excitement bubbled from every room. The whole house seemed to be watching and waiting, buoyed up by the whispers and giggles of the performers, the anticipation of the parents, the shouts of laughter from the younger members of the audience and the repeated cries of 'Merry Christmas' that echoed through the corridors. It was the sound of happiness, and it escaped out through the front door and wrapped itself round each new arrival.

Abi's mum dropped the four friends at the door. Miss Flood had asked the volunteers to be half an hour early, so they were good and ready when the guests started to arrive. As the girls walked through the front door, however, it was clear that lots of people had decided to come early and enjoy the pre-show fun because the reception area was crowded. The girls grinned at each other as they soaked up the buzz of the excitement, then they made their way to the desk.

Daniel and Jack were working hard behind the desk, selling tickets and directing people to the cloakroom area and the refreshments. They looked up as the girls approached, and stopped in their tracks.

'Wow!' Jack exclaimed. 'You all look gorgeous.'

Daniel didn't say anything but just stared at Sarah and blushed.

'You look pretty decent yourselves,' Hannah joked – the boys were wearing shirts and ties specially for the occasion.

'What can we do?' Grace asked, immediately getting into her busy stride.

'Well, some help here would be welcome,' Jack said, looking over her shoulder as more guests spilled through the doorway behind them. 'And I'd say we need someone posted at the top of the corridor to the ballroom and someone else at the double doors, to encourage everyone to go in and sit down. Otherwise we'll never get started.'

'No problem,' Grace said. 'I'll stay here with you two. Do you want to join me Hannah? And maybe Sarah and Abi can take the other two posts.'

The girls split up. Sarah couldn't help noticing how delighted Jack looked that Grace had opted to man the desk alongside him and Daniel. She and Abi made their way through the bodies and over to the ballroom corridor.

'I'll stay up here,' Sarah offered, 'and send them down to you at the door.'

'Don't forget to check for tickets,' Abi reminded her, 'they all need to pay to get in.'

'Will do,' Sarah said.

Once she was on her own, without Abi, Grace and Hannah at her side, Sarah felt a bit strange in her grown-up dress. She'd had to wear stiff velvet dresses for piano recitals in the past, but she'd never scrubbed up like this before. Normally, she felt almost invisible as she went about, but tonight she felt much more conspicuous.

The photograph of Felicity was standing on a big easel and alongside it was the poster of her invite. As people started to drift Sarah's way, many of them asked about the young ballerina. She explained the significance of the night – the sixth anniversary of Felicity's death – and that a special performance would mark it. It added a real element of interest – most of the parents would have sat through many a ballet performance by their children, but hearing about the link to Felicity and that it was to be celebrated in a unique way, well, Sarah could tell they were intrigued and eager for the show to start.

More and more people began to make their way towards Sarah, who took their tickets, and then on down the corridor to Abi. She directed them into the ballroom, smiling at the gasps of delight as they entered and were met by Grace's fantastic vision and the eerily lit stage. The room looked incredible and Grace was proved right – the Christmas-themed colour scheme was an absolute hit.

Abi saw Marcella Roseman bustling about up at the stage area – she was marshalling all the dancers to the backstage areas and ensuring everything was ready. The screen was hidden up in the rigging because Mia and Felicity's dance was going to be the last dance of the evening – the grand finale.

By five minutes to curtain up, the whole audience was in the ballroom and seated, ready and waiting. Abi left her post and joined Sarah.

'I saw Mr Grainger come in – on his own,' she said.

'Yeah, I know,' Sarah said. 'Simone didn't come after all.'

'We'll talk to her soon,' Abi promised. 'She can't avoid us forever. Once we have tonight done and Felicity is happy, we'll be free to think about other things for a change.'

'Come on,' Sarah said, 'let's join the others.'

The volunteers were gathered in the reception, where Jack was storing all the tickets and money in the strong box, locking it away safely. Sarah looked around at their little group.

'Did Chrissy and Elaine not turn up?' she asked, surprised that they would miss Sophie's big night.

Daniel shook his head. 'I haven't see them anyway.'

From behind Sarah came the sound of Chrissy's

voice, oozing sweetness. 'Oh Daniel, have you been missing me?'

They all spun round, and there in the doorway stood Chrissy and Elaine. All eight volunteers stood and stared. Chrissy must have spent a fortune on her outfit because it looked like a designer evening gown. It was grey silk, which looked beautiful against her glossy black curls. She was wearing a fur stole to keep out the night's chill *and* she was wearing actual high heels. Her necklace and bracelet must have been borrowed from her mother because they looked expensive – and real.

'I can guess who this grand entrance is aimed at,' Sarah whispered out of the side of her mouth to Hannah. Her heart sank as she looked Chrissy up and down. If Daniel was going to dance with anyone tonight, it had to be Chrissy – she looked incredible, easily the best dressed girl there.

Chrissy and Elaine sashayed across the room, and Sarah took some pleasure in seeing how hard Chrissy had to concentrate to walk in her high shoes. She fluttered her eyelashes at Daniel, who was standing rooted to the spot, and said, 'Now, you're not going to charge *me* to go in, are you?' Then she laughed a fluty, silly, girly laugh that set Sarah's teeth on edge.

'It's time to go in,' Josh said, deliberately not remarking on how Chrissy looked. 'It's about to start.'

The volunteers all made their way down the

corridor and into the ballroom, taking up their seats in the last row. As they settled themselves, Hannah whispered to Sarah, 'Have you seen her yet?'

'Who?' Sarah whispered back.

'Felicity, of course,' Hannah replied. 'It would be awful if she didn't come.'

'No, I haven't seen anything,' Sarah whispered as the lights in the ballroom dimmed.

It hadn't occurred to her that Felicity might back out of the dance, but now that Hannah said it, it did seem strange that they hadn't seen any sign of her at all. What if she hadn't seen the invite? What if she was too scared to go through with it? If she didn't turn up, she would lose her chance to find peace.

I wonder what happens then, Sarah thought anxiously. *Could she get stuck here forever?*

17

The Final Dance

One by one the scenes were played out. The dancers outdid themselves, putting their hearts into every step. The 'backstage' area worked beautifully, with dancers suddenly appearing on stage when the lights came up, without fuss or noise to announce their arrival. It was clear that the audience was really impressed by the whole performance.

When the second to last scene ended, Marcella's voice announced a ten-minute interval to prepare for the finale – in which Felicity was meant to appear.

'I still haven't seen her,' Sarah whispered urgently to her friends. They all looked worried now. 'Let's go find Mia and see if Felicity is about.'

They slipped out of their seats and made their way out of the ballroom. Once outside, they ran around to the door to the ante-room and knocked.

'Come in,' called Mia.

They stepped in and closed the door behind them. Mia looked nervous as she retouched her stage make-up. 'Hi, you lot,' she said, 'is everything ready for the dance?'

'We haven't seen her yet,' Abi admitted.

Mia's face dropped. 'You don't think she'll stay away, do you?' she asked, sounding hugely disappointed.

'Let's hope not,' Sarah said under her breath.

They watched as Mia finished her make-up, then began jumping up and down on the spot very gracefully, to ensure her muscles were warmed up. Suddenly, the air in the room became colder and started to shimmer. Sarah breathed a huge sigh of relief. This time, even Mia noticed the change.

'Is she here now?' she asked quickly.

Felicity was standing next to the door that led to the hidden corridor. She nodded at the girls and managed a small smile.

'She's here, yes,' Hannah replied. 'And she's ready.'

Felicity was staring intently at Mia, focusing all of her energy on her. Sarah watched, fascinated, as Mia seemed to sense the ghost's presence. She slowly turned her head and looked at the spot where Felicity was standing.

'Is she over there?' she asked in wonder.

'Yes, at the door,' Sarah replied. 'Can you sense her?' she asked.

'I . . . I think so,' Mia said, looking puzzled. 'I feel like someone is watching me.' She stepped towards the door and whispered, 'Felicity? Are you happy to do this? I hope so much that it will work.'

Felicity never took her eyes from Mia's face. She looked like she was struggling to control her emotions, like she might cry at any moment. Then she raised her hand and stretched it out towards Mia's face. She didn't touch her, but Mia suddenly gasped and raised her own hand to her cheek.

'I feel a coldness,' she whispered.

The girls looked at each other, unsure as to what exactly was happening.

'She's reaching out to you,' Sarah said quietly.

'Felicity, I'm so sorry you had that accident,' Mia said, her voice soft with emotion. 'I wish you were still here.'

Sarah felt a lump forming in her throat and tears at the back of her eyes. Felicity looked so young, and Mia looked so sad – it was hard to watch. Sarah was lost in the moment and she jumped when Felicity said her name.

'Sarah, tell Mia that I am sorry.'

'Mia, she wants you to know that she is sorry.'

'There's no need for sorry,' Mia replied. 'It's all water under the bridge now.'

'No, it's not,' Felicity said, her voice stronger now. Sarah shook her head, to show Mia that the ghost disagreed. 'Tell Mia that I am really, really sorry for being so horrible to her. I was wrong and I wish I could go back and make it different, but

I can't. I knew what her mother was like because she was just like mine. We could have been friends and helped each other, but instead I bullied her and made her even more miserable. I'm so ashamed, Mia,' Felicity said, reaching her hand out again, 'and so sorry. Please forgive me.'

Sarah had to wipe away tears as she repeated Felicity's message. She felt Hannah taking her hand and was glad of the contact. There was so much emotion in the room, it felt like all the air had been sucked out of it. Hannah held Grace's hand on the other side, and Grace took Abi's hand.

Mia listened carefully to Felicity's words spoken by Sarah. She nodded slowly. 'I forgive you, Felicity,' she whispered.

The ghost's shoulders sagged and the air around her shimmered softly. She exhaled a deep breath, and it sounded like pain leaving her body. 'Thank you,' she said.

'She thanked you,' Sarah said to Mia.

Mia smiled. 'And I want to thank you, Felicity, for coming back. I have learned so much from all this. But now I want you to find peace.' She reached out her hand in the direction of her invisible friend, and Felicity reached her hand towards it. 'Are you ready for our final dance?'

Sarah, Abi, Hannah and Grace made their way back to the ballroom, feeling drained by all they had just witnessed. It had seemed so impossible that they could ever help Felicity, but now they had seen the weight fall from her shoulders when Mia gave her forgiveness. The four girls walked hand in hand all the way back, unable to say anything to each other just yet. At the double doors to the ballroom they let go of each other's hands and crept quietly back into the room, finding their seats noiselessly.

Marcella Roseman's voice sounded across the PA system once more, announcing the last scene of the night. A hum of anticipation ran through the ballroom. The stage lights went off and the room was plunged into darkness, with only the dim glow of the fairy lights in the glass bowls arranged by Grace. The audience fell quiet; no one moved.

When the stage lights came on again, the long screen was pulled down to its full extent and next to it stood a girl wearing a hooded black cloak that covered her body – only her pale face was visible in the spotlight. It was Mia.

'Tonight, I will dance the dance that never was,' she said, her voice firm and sure. 'Six years ago to this night, I should have danced this ballet with my fellow ballerina, Felicity Fenston. As most of you know, Felicity was involved in an accident that night and she died. We have all missed her, especially in the academy, where she was the star pupil. To honour her memory and her achievements, I am going to perform a tribute to her. I will dance the part of the Witch, and I ask you all to picture Felicity dancing the part of Snow White.'

Mia retreated into the shadows beyond the spotlight. Slowly, the lights fanned out to gently illuminate the left-hand side of the stage. Mia began to dance, her movements strong and graceful, her face expressing all the jealousy and anger of the wicked witch, her gestures enticing Snow White to eat the apple she offered. It was a mesmerizing performance.

Suddenly, the screen flickered into life. There was a gasp of recognition as Felicity's image appeared. She was dressed in the Snow White costume, her little face a picture of determination and concentration. It was the dress rehearsal for the performance six years ago. She began to move with great elegance, dancing out the story of Snow White, responding to Mia's movements on the other side of the stage. Sarah watched as the people around her were completely caught up in the spectacle, their mouths falling open, their eyes wide. It looked so strange and yet so beautiful – the real dancer and the projected dancer, moving together, joined by the dance.

The audience couldn't see the rest of the picture, though. On the stage, Felicity danced close to Mia, her movements mimicking those of her projected image. She was lost in the dance, her face lit up with a joy the four friends had never seen there before. For the girls, the three dancers moved in unison. It was an incredible sight.

A movement by the doors to the ballroom caught Sarah's eye and distracted her. She peered into the darkness and made out a person standing at the door, back pressed to the wall. It took her a moment to realize that it was Simone. Sarah smiled – *She came after all. Now she'll get to see this too.* As she looked at her, she saw Simone's shoulders move in little jerks. *What's she doing?* A moment later, Sarah realized that Simone was crying quietly as she looked at the two dancers on the stage.

When the dance ended, the screen went still and held a final shot of Felicity. There was a few seconds of spellbound silence, then the audience thundered an applause, jumping out of their seats, their faces glowing like they'd just witnessed a miracle. It was deafening – even Mia looked taken aback as she swept to her feet and prepared to curtsy. She spread her arms to the side and as she did so, Felicity put her hand in hers and they dropped to curtsy together.

That was the final straw – Sarah, Abi, Grace and Hannah burst into tears at almost the same moment. When Sarah looked over at the doors to find Simone, the space where she'd been standing was empty. Simone was gone.

It took a while to get the audience out of the ballroom so they could rearrange the chairs and prepare for the supper dance. Everyone seemed reluctant to leave when they had just enjoyed such a wonderful performance – like they were trying to hold on to it for as long as possible. But, with Marcella ordering them about, they soon got the message and went outside. The volunteers and the dancers quickly set about pushing the chairs against the walls, while Marcella's sister and her team set up trestle tables and filled them with dishes of food. It only took about fifteen minutes, then the lights were softened, the doors were opened and the guests streamed back in.

The girls looked about anxiously for Mia and eventually she emerged from behind the stage, her face scrubbed of make-up and wearing a pretty tea dress. She came straight over to them, her eyes still shining.

'Wasn't that amazing?' she said, hugging them in turn.

'Seriously?' said Sarah. 'I think that's probably the most amazing thing I've ever seen.'

'You were brilliant,' Abi said with admiration. 'You're such a good dancer.'

'I'll never forget this,' Mia said, smiling at them. 'Thanks for letting me be part of it. It was such an experience.'

'You were the reason for it,' Hannah said, 'you were always part of it, you just didn't know.'

'Simone saw it too,' Sarah said quietly. 'She was really moved by it, but then she left.'

Mia nodded, but said nothing.

There was the sound of waltz-style music, and couples began to take to the floor for the dancing.

'I'm going to go look for Mum,' Mia said, 'and see if I can help Auntie Flora. I'll catch you all later. Bye.'

The four friends went over to the chairs at the back of the room and sat down. They could leave the refreshments to the restaurant people, so really their work was done now.

'What a night!' Grace said with a sigh. 'Just magical.'

'I thought I was going to pass out when the image came up on the screen,' Abi said, shaking her head. 'She looked so beautiful, didn't she?'

They nodded and smiled at the memory of the dance.

'And now she's danced Snow White,' Sarah said with a smile, 'so she should be able to find peace at last. Go, the ghost detectives!'

They laughed, then Hannah suddenly gripped Sarah's arm hard.

'Ow!' Sarah cried. 'What the –'

'Look!' Hannah hissed. 'Miss Flood.'

They all looked out on the dance floor and there was Miss Flood, dancing in the arms of Mr Daven, the third-class teacher. The girls made faces at each other and started giggling.

'And go, Miss Flood!' Sarah declared.

The floor was filled with dancers now, and the girls watched them sway around the room.

'I suppose there'll be no chance of a bit of Lady Gaga, will there?' Grace asked.

'Not on your nelly,' Hannah replied, laughing. 'This is dancing for the oldies.'

As they watched, two all too familiar faces materialized in the crowd and walked towards them: Chrissy and Elaine. They stopped not far from the girls and Chrissy regarded them with a haughty grin.

'Nice try on the dressing up, girls,' she said snidely. 'Pity it didn't work out so well for you.' She grabbed Elaine's arm and the two of them sniggered and walked over to join Tiffany and Sophie, who were sitting on chairs along the centre of the wall.

'You know,' said Sarah, as she watched them take their seats and shoot triumphant glances in the girls' direction, 'maybe we should just feel sorry for Chrissy and be nice to her.'

'What?' Abi demanded, shocked. 'Why does she deserve any of us being nice to her? She's horrible with a capital H.'

'I'll never forgive her for embarrassing you,' Sarah said fiercely, 'or for the time she upset me about my dad, but I'm just thinking about Felicity. She was a bully, but it was because of the other stuff going on her life. Maybe Chrissy has other stuff going on too. She might be like Felicity and end up having to live with the guilt of being mean to so many people. That's all I'm saying.'

Her three friends looked down along the line of chairs at Chrissy and the Clones. It was hard to imagine Chrissy having weak spots, but then, who knew what another person was thinking or feeling?

'You might be right,' Grace conceded, 'but I just can't see myself being all nicey-nicey to her somehow. I mean, you're hurting about your dad, but I don't see you taking it out on everyone else.'

Sarah stared down at her hands. It wasn't nice to be reminded of her dad, but she appreciated what Grace was saying.

'Boy at twelve o'clock,' Hannah said in a quiet voice.

Sarah looked up, confused. 'What?'

'Boy at twelve o'clock,' Hannah hissed.

Sarah, Abi and Grace followed her gaze, and they saw Jack coming towards them. He looked nervous.

'Oh!' Sarah said with a grin.

'Hi,' Jack said as he reached them. He fiddled with his tie, then turned to Grace. 'Erm, Grace, do you fancy a dance? I'm not very good and this music is awful, but I thought we could give it a go.'

Grace went bright red and looked astounded. 'Me?' she said in a squeaky voice.

'Yep,' Jack said, nodding. 'If you want to.'

'Oh right, yeah,' Grace said, her voice still sounding too high. 'Sure. I'm no good either, but we can do our best.'

Jack held out his hand and Grace took it and he led her off to the middle of the floor. Abi, Hannah and Sarah giggled and made faces at each other.

'I knew he liked her,' Sarah said.

'He's really brave,' Abi replied, 'I'd hate to walk all the way across the floor and ask someone to dance. I'd be in a sweat.'

'I think he was,' Hannah said, laughing. 'Good on him, though. Oh crikey, don't look now, but here's another one.'

Solomon was making his way towards them, looking distinctly uncomfortable. He stopped in front of Hannah's chair, but words seemed to fail him. Hannah looked at him questioningly.

'Did you want to dance, Sol?' she asked.

He nodded wordlessly.

'We can dance,' Hannah said with a grin, 'but you've got to promise to talk to me.'

Solomon smiled gratefully at her and nodded again. 'Sounds good,' he said, then took her hand and led her off.

Sarah moved over to the seat next to Abi and they hunched over together.

'Well, had you guessed Sol liked Hannah?' Abi asked. 'Because I hadn't.'

'No, he's so quiet, I never thought about it,' Sarah said.

'I think they look cute together,' Abi said. Suddenly, her face changed from a smile to an expression of something between surprise and fear. Sarah almost didn't dare look up this time to see what Abi was looking at. When she did, she understood: Josh was walking across the floor towards them.

'Abi, stay calm,' Sarah said urgently, afraid that her friend would start hyperventilating at any moment.

Josh stood in front of Abi, but before he could speak, there was a burst of loud laughter from where Chrissy and her friends were sitting. Josh took a deep breath and ignored them.

'Abi,' he said, looking straight at her, 'will you dance with me?'

Abi's eyes flicked in Chrissy's direction and she stammered, 'I-I . . . I . . .'

Josh's eyes never left Abi's face. 'I think it's the best way to show everyone that we don't care about Chrissy and her gossip,' he said quietly.

Sarah watched Abi and she knew her friend really wanted to dance with Josh.

Go on, Abi, she willed her, *go on*.

Abi gave a curt nod, as if she'd just convinced herself of something, then she smiled at Josh and stood up. She put her hand in his. 'I'd love to, Josh, that would be awesome,' she said. Holding her head high, she marched off with him on to the dance floor.

Go, Abi! Sarah cheered inwardly.

Sarah sat happily on her chair, tapping her feet to the music and watching her friends dancing and chatting. She heard the sound of high heels clip-clopping on the wooden floor and looked up to see Chrissy and her friends coming towards her. They stopped just one chair away from her and sat down.

'You looked like you needed company,' Chrissy said meanly, 'seeing as *no one* wants to dance with you.'

Sarah tried out her new tactics and smiled widely. 'Thanks, Chrissy, that is *so* nice of you to think of me.'

Chrissy glared at her and turned back to her friends, whispering in a huddle with them. Sarah saw Abi, Hannah and Grace all looking over, as if they might run to the rescue at any moment. She gave them a little wave to show that she was fine. As she did so, she saw Daniel across the room and her heart skipped a beat. He began to walk towards her.

Then Elaine whispered loudly, 'Here he comes, Chrissy!'

Sarah looked at the ground and felt like a fool – of course, he was walking over to Chrissy. She kept her eyes down, folding and refolding the fabric of her dress across her knee. She heard his footsteps, then out of the corner of her eye she saw Chrissy rising up out of her seat. She stood there expectantly, but Daniel finished his walk in front of Sarah.

'Would you like to dance?' he said, holding out his hand.

Sarah could see his hand, and she slowly raised her eyes until she was looking at his face. 'You're asking me?' she said faintly.

He nodded and smiled at her.

'Sure,' she replied, hoping her legs would hold her when she stood up. She placed her hand in his and he led her in among the dancers. She chanced a quick glance in Chrissy's direction and saw her sitting down again, her face flaming.

Sarah smiled shyly at Daniel. 'I think you may have upset Chrissy just a little bit,' she murmured.

He grinned at her and bent his head towards her ear. 'What revenge do you think she'll come up with for us? Do you think we'll find a picture of us dancing on the noticeboard in school?'

Sarah grinned back. 'No, she'll probably take it out on me, you'll be glad to hear. She's never liked me anyway. I'll be like the decoy, keeping you safe.'

Daniel laughed and out of the corner of her eye, Sarah saw Chrissy scowling fiercely. 'I like the idea of my own decoy,' he said, teasing her. 'I'll have to keep you close to me from now.'

Sarah looked quickly at him, then down at the

floor, blushing deeply. She tried to think of something witty to say, but her brain failed her completely. All she could think was, *I'm dancing with Daniel, I'm dancing with Daniel* and the words played on, over and over, keeping time with the music.

18

Guilt

It was Christmas Eve and the girls had gathered in Sarah's house to exchange their gifts. Sarah knew her mother wanted to keep the house filled with people as much as possible, so it didn't feel like the three of them rattling around on their own. She had asked Abi, Hannah and Grace to come over and do their present-giving there. It was freezing cold outside, and the girls were very happy to sit by the fire in Sarah's living room to catch up on the events of Saturday night.

'Did you see Chrissy's face when Daniel asked Sarah to dance?' Grace said with a wicked grin. 'I wish I'd had a camera at that moment.'

Sarah smiled at the memory.

'Now *that* would have been a good photo for the school noticeboard!' Abi joked, making them all laugh.

'I wish Felicity had come to say goodbye to us, though,' Hannah said. 'It would have been nice to see her one last time.'

'I'm just glad she finally got what she needed,' Sarah replied. 'All these years feeling so bad about herself – it must be a huge weight off her mind to feel at peace at last.'

Her friends nodded. They were so pleased that they had finally figured out how to help Felicity.

'Right then,' said Grace, rubbing her hands together, 'present time!'

Before they could pull out each other's presents, there was a blur of noise as four different mobile-phone ringtones sounded loudly. They looked at each other in surprise.

'Someone wishing us all a Merry Christmas?' Sarah asked.

They grabbed their phones and looked at the message.

'Wow,' Grace said, 'I hadn't expected that.'

'No, me either,' Hannah agreed. 'I thought we'd have to pester her into seeing us.'

'She means right now, doesn't she?' Sarah groaned. 'It's so cold out there.'

The message sounded urgent:

Hi. Sorry to ask on Christmas Eve, but I really need to talk to you. Can you meet me at the museum? How soon can you be here? SG

'I don't fancy going all the way up there either,' Grace said, 'but Simone wouldn't ask unless it was important – especially not at the moment when she's barely speaking to us anyway.' She tapped her phone quickly and let Simone know they'd be there in twenty-five minutes.

Sarah groaned again. 'We work way too hard,' she grumbled.

'Come on, you,' Hannah said, poking her playfully, 'a bit of exercise will do us good.'

'All right,' Sarah sighed. 'I suppose I am curious why she's suddenly keen to get in touch. I'll just go let my mum know that we're going out for a while.'

Mrs Forde was surprised that the girls wanted to leave the fire and cycle off in the cold, but she just told them to wrap up warmly and be back by five o'clock. They layered themselves in coats, scarves, hats and gloves, then went out to climb on to their bikes and cycle to the museum.

When they got there, they could see lights on in the downstairs rooms. Simone had obviously let herself in.

I wonder what she's up to, Sarah thought. *Why didn't she want to meet at the gate lodge?*

They wheeled their bikes into the stands but didn't bother to lock them – they were definitely the only people up there that day. Then they pushed open the front door and stepped inside.

'Simone?' Hannah called. 'Are you here?'

'Coming,' a voice called from somewhere near the

back stairs. They heard the sound of quick footsteps and Simone walked into the hallway. She looked pale and upset, like she was looking for something important she had lost but couldn't find it.

'You OK, Simone?' Sarah asked, feeling a bit worried about her.

Simone looked at her distractedly. 'Oh yeah, fine,' she said. 'Thanks for coming. I feel bad that it's Christmas Eve and you should be, you know . . .' Her voice trailed off as if she was thinking of something else entirely.

Sarah decided this was no time to beat around the bush. 'Simone, you're acting like a complete weirdo,' she stated bluntly. 'You haven't talked to us for weeks, you've been really odd and now you call us here on a day when you should be with your dad. What's going on? What's been bothering you?'

Simone managed a weak smile. 'Straight to the point as usual, Sarah.' She clasped her hands together, twisting the fingers round each other in that nervous way Sarah had noticed before. 'It's just that,' she began, then took a deep breath, 'it's just that, I need your help.'

'No problem,' Abi said immediately. 'What can we do?'

'I need to speak to Felicity,' Simone said in a low voice. 'I tried to do it without you,' she said in a rush, 'I was here for hours yesterday and again all morning, walking through the rooms, calling her name, but there's no sign of her. I need to talk to her.'

Simone looked so desperate that Sarah felt sorry for her. She looked over at Abi, Hannah and Grace, knowing that one of them was going to have to tell Simone the truth. Sarah was very grateful when she saw Hannah move towards Simone. Hannah put her hand on Simone's arm and looked her in the eye. 'I'm so sorry,' she said gently, 'but after Felicity performed the final dance she was freed of her guilt about Mia and, well, she's gone, Simone.'

Simone looked stricken, her eyes wide with panic. 'No, she can't be. I can't be too late.' She covered her face with her hands.

The four girls looked at each other, at a loss as to what to do now.

'Can we help?' Abi asked her. 'Can you talk to us about whatever it is?'

Simone shook her head without removing her hands from her face. 'It doesn't matter,' she whispered through her fingers.

'It looks like it matters a lot,' Sarah remarked.

'It's my own fault for being such a coward,' Simone said hopelessly.

Suddenly, Sarah saw a flickering light out of the corner of her eye. She turned, and she saw that the air was shimmering between her and Simone. Her mouth fell open. *We're getting another one already*, she thought wildly.

The air cleared and there stood Felicity. She was still dressed in her ballet costume, but she looked very different now – softer and calmer, with a glow that hadn't been there before.

Sarah couldn't help herself. 'You seriously have to be kidding me! Please tell me there's no more for us to do for you?'

Abi, Hannah and Grace looked over and gasped when they saw who it was – and what Sarah had said to her. To their surprise, Felicity simply started giggling.

'Good to see you too, Sarah,' she teased.

Sarah recovered her wits and immediately started to apologize. 'Sorry, Felicity, I didn't mean to sound so rude, I just thought, you know, you were at peace and all that. We got you to the dance, didn't we?'

'Yes, you did,' Felicity said, smiling. 'And it was the best night ever. I loved every minute of it.'

'So why are you still here?' Sarah wailed.

'Ask Simone,' Felicity said, turning to look at Simone, who was standing clutching Hannah's hand, staring in the direction where Sarah was directing her comments. Simone's hand flew to her mouth in shock.

'Is she here?' she asked.

'She's here all right,' Sarah said with an edge to her voice. 'But we don't know why. She said to ask you.'

Simone's pale face reddened and her eyes filled

with tears. 'She's here for me. To tell me the truth.'

The girls looked from Simone to the ghost and back again.

Felicity smiled at Simone and said to Sarah, 'Tell her that I am here for her. I didn't know that until now. I tried to leave after the performance, but I couldn't. I heard her calling me, but she couldn't see me. There's something we have to talk about before all this can be finished properly. Then I can go.'

Sarah repeated Felicity's words to Simone and waited for her to reply.

Finally, she thought, *we're going to find out what all this is about.*

Simone looked like a condemned man at the guillotine. Slowly, she began to speak, looking in the direction where Felicity was standing, waiting patiently.

'Felicity, I caused your death. I've known it all these years and it's haunted me every single day since the accident.'

The four girls were rooted to the spot, shocked silent by what Simone was saying.

'It was me who put the note in your locker,' Simone said, her voice sounding like it was coming from somewhere far away. 'I didn't want to hurt you, but I couldn't bear to see you being like that to Mia. In the weeks before the performance, you were so horrible to her and I just couldn't take it. I thought if I let you know how it was affecting her, you'd stop. So I put that note in your locker on the day of the performance and I saw you take it out and read it. Then you didn't turn up –' Simone's voice caught on the words, but she forced herself to continue – 'and then they told us you'd been in an accident. You weren't even on the way to the academy – you were running away somewhere. You were running away because I had written those things. I know that's what it was. You'd have been safe at the academy if it hadn't been for the note. It was my fault.'

Felicity was watching her closely as she spoke, but her face didn't show anger or shock. Instead, as Simone poured her heart out, describing all the feelings that had trapped her for so long, Felicity just looked incredibly sad. When Simone finished, Felicity turned to Sarah.

'Sarah, it's very important that you tell Simone what I'm about to say word for word. I want you to tell her as I talk.'

Felicity began to talk, and Sarah repeated every sentence exactly as she spoke it.

'Simone, I know now that there were two reasons I couldn't rest in peace – the guilt I felt at how I treated Mia and the guilt you felt at how you thought you treated me. I've been crushed by it ever since that day, and so have you. So now I'm here to tell you the truth. Simone, it was not your fault. It's not your fault. I did read the note, and

I actually admired you for being such a good friend to Mia. I was a bit jealous because I didn't have a best friend. But I knew what you said was true – that I had been making Mia's life miserable and it wasn't right. I didn't run off in a huff, though, or because I was upset or anything like that. I wanted to say sorry to Mia and I thought the best way to do that was to not turn up that night, so the scout from the ballet school would only see Mia dance – and she'd get the place.'

Simone was listening intently and now tears began to spill down her cheeks. 'But why were you on that road?' she said hoarsely.

'I knew if my mother found me, she'd haul me straight to the academy. I wanted to stay out of her way until the show was over. So I just went walking. I wasn't thinking about where I was going. I was just hiding out really. And then there was the car and the sound of the brakes . . .' Felicity looked down at her ballet shoes, then raised her head again. 'It was an accident, that's all. And I was on that road because that's where I wanted to be, not because of your note.'

Simone made a sound that sounded like grief, then she collapsed into Hannah's arms, crying loudly.

'You didn't cause anything,' Felicity said firmly. 'It was just meant to be. That was my time. That's all.'

Sarah was speaking Felicity's words, but at the same time her brain was churning with them. A wave of emotion swept over her as she listened to Felicity and looked at Simone. She knew exactly what it felt like to carry a secret that hurt. There was something she had wanted to confide in her mum so often, but it was like her mouth was sealed shut whenever she tried. Tears poured down Sarah's face.

Abi and Grace were caught between Simone and Sarah, staring from one to the other in disbelief. After a few seconds, they rushed to Sarah and wrapped their arms round her.

'What is it, Sarah?' Simone asked through her own tears.

Sarah looked at her friends and knew she could trust them. 'I thought I was the reason my dad left,' she said quietly through her tears. 'I've thought it for a long time and it's been eating me up inside.' She gulped. 'We had a big fight one day in the summer and I said . . . I said –' she fought back the tears so she could finish – 'I said I wished he'd just go away somewhere and not always be in the way, causing Mum to be unhappy.' She looked at her friends with wide sad eyes. 'I didn't mean it,' she whispered, 'but then he left.'

Abi, Grace, Hannah and Simone engulfed her in hugs, telling her she wasn't to blame, that she loved her dad, that he loved her, that it was nothing to do with her, that they loved her. Sarah cried and laughed all at once, hugging them tightly in return.

Standing on her own, Felicity watched them, smiling. Eventually, she coughed to get their attention. They all turned to her.

'Thank you so much for helping me, all of you,' she said, looking at Simone too. 'You girls will be glad to hear that I'm done now. I think we've all found a bit of peace today,' she said with a smile. 'I have to say goodbye now.'

The air shimmered round her once more, and Felicity disappeared.

19

Making Amends

'Please tell me,' Sarah said as she wiped away the last of her tears, 'that Beryl wrote out a ritual for how to stop being a ghost detective?'

Simone laughed and shook her head. 'Not that I know of,' she replied. 'Once you do the ritual, that's pretty much it – the ghosts will come when they want to. Anyway, I'm very, very grateful that you lot did the ritual in the first place. It's led to this, today.' She smiled at them.

'I'm really glad too,' Abi said, squeezing her hand. 'I can't believe you went around thinking like that for so long, Simone.'

'It just seemed the only explanation,' Simone said. 'Once I believed it was my fault, I couldn't stop believing it. And I felt so awful and guilty about it. I couldn't handle it.'

'You poor thing,' Grace said, still trying to come to terms with all that had just happened.

'No wonder we couldn't figure out how to help Felicity,' Hannah said, shaking her head, 'it was a web of things, wasn't it? We expected one simple solution, but it was so different.'

'You did it in the end, though,' Simone said with a smile. 'You're good at this, you have to admit.'

'I still say if I find a way of undoing it, I'm resigning,' Sarah said firmly.

'So what now?' Grace asked. 'We've got another hour or so before we have to get back. How about you stand us a hot chocolate by the fire at the gate lodge, Simone?'

'Absolutely,' Simone agreed. 'You've earned it. First, though, there's something I want to do, but I need your help again.'

'I thought we'd already earned the hot chocolate?' Sarah teased her.

'Oh, you have, but I've just one more job for you.'

'OK, what is it?' Sarah asked.

'I need to get in touch with Mia,' Simone said quietly. 'I have to tell her about this and explain why I dropped her as a friend so suddenly.'

She didn't need to say another word. Sarah took out her phone, pulled up Mia's number and handed it to Simone. 'There you go. Press call and you'll be on to her.'

'Thanks,' Simone said, then she moved off to make the call.

The four friends watched her leave, then turned to each other.

'Another crazy day in our crazy lives,' Grace said, attempting an American accent like Abi's.

'I really hope we don't have anyone else looking for help for a while,' Abi said with a sigh, 'I can't take all this emotion. I'm worn out!'

'It's been an adventure, all right,' Hannah replied. 'I feel like Alice going through the looking glass or something. Or maybe more like Lyra in *Northern Lights*, you know, stepping into strange worlds. Or maybe even –'

Sarah sighed. 'Hannah! You're making my head ache.'

The four friends burst out laughing, and Simone smiled at them as she rejoined them. 'What's so funny?' she asked.

'Hannah's bookworm tendencies,' Sarah said drily. 'That was a quick call,' she said as she took her phone back from Simone. 'Was she not there?'

'She was,' Simone replied, 'but she said she wanted to talk in person. She's on her way here.'

'Now?' Sarah said, surprised. 'Do you make a habit of calling people out of their houses on Christmas Eve? I just want to know so I'm warned for next year!'

Simone laughed – like her old self. 'Not usually, no,' she joked. 'I'm making an exception this year.'

While they waited for Mia to arrive, the five girls talked over the events of the past weeks, filling each other in on everything. Sarah watched Simone talking and laughing, and she knew Mr Grainger had been right: Simone did like having them as friends. She thought about how lonely Simone must have been since cutting herself off from everyone, and she hoped hearing the truth from Felicity would mean that Simone could start again.

After about twenty minutes, there was a knock at the front door and Grace walked over to let Mia in. She stepped inside looking a bit shy and uncertain.

'Hi, everyone,' she said. 'Merry Christmas.' She swung her backpack off her back and unbuckled it. 'I have a little present for you,' she said and took out four envelopes. On each was written a name: Abi, Sarah, Grace, Hannah. She handed them to the girls. 'I was hoping I'd see you soon, so I could get these to you.' She smiled warmly at them, then noticed Simone standing behind them, holding back. 'Hey, Simone,' she said with a smile. 'I'm really glad you called me.'

Simone nodded. 'I wanted to tell you some things,' she said.

'Wow!' Grace shouted suddenly. 'Look,' she said, pointing to the window, 'it's started snowing.'

'You're not going to break into song, are you?' Sarah said in a horrified tone.

Grace stuck out her tongue at her. 'No, but I am going to suggest that we give Mia and Simone a bit of space and go outside for a little while to enjoy it while it's falling.'

'Good idea,' Hannah said, and the four of them made their way outside. They walked to the edge of the driveway where it met the grass. There was a bench there, placed to face the house. They sat in a row, huddled together for warmth.

'I wouldn't exactly call this snow, Grace,' Abi said with a grin. 'I think you'd need to come to America to see an actual snowfall.'

'This is good enough for me,' Grace said in delight. 'If it sticks, I'll be very happy!'

Soft snowflakes drifted down from the grey sky above, gently making their way to the ground and on to the girls' clothes. It was all very quiet. The house rose up in front of them, gazing sternly out on the parkland behind them. It felt like they were the only four people in the world.

'Has anyone opened their envelope?' Abi asked.

No one had. Now, they ripped them open at the same time. Each envelope contained the same thing: a large photograph of Mia and Felicity's ballet performance, showing Mia and the projected image of Felicity caught in a similar pose. The girls looked at it in silence for a few moments.

'I'm going to put it in my diary,' Hannah said finally. 'It'll finish the story nicely.'

Grace looked from the photograph, up to the house. 'Hey, do you remember what Miss Flood wrote on the list when she first invited people to volunteer?'

Her friends looked at her, not sure what she was getting at.

'She promised those who volunteered an unforgettable experience,' Grace said, smiling at them. 'That has to be the understatement of the century, doesn't it?'

Abi laughed. 'Pretty much,' she agreed. 'You know, I just can't believe my luck that my mom moved us all here and I met you guys and got to know this place. I just love it like crazy now. I can see myself working in this museum until I'm ancient.'

'We'll put you on display as a fossil,' Hannah joked.

'Seriously, though,' Sarah said, 'it's true, isn't it? This place really does get under your skin. I find myself thinking about it so much – things we can do, how we can make it better – all that stuff. I never would have thought I'd be into a museum.'

The snow continued to fall as the friends looked at the Grainger house and thought about all the strange things that had happened within its walls. First Beryl and now they were having an incredible adventure because of this house.

'It's kind of magical,' Grace said.

'The snow?' Hannah asked her.

'No, the place, the house,' Grace replied, pointing at it. 'All this. I think there's some kind of magic at work here.'

The light in the sitting room went off suddenly.

One by one, the lights on the ground floor went out and the house fell into darkness. The front door opened and they watched Mia and Simone step outside and Simone pull the door closed behind her, then lock it. She turned to Mia and they smiled at each other.

'So what about next year?' Sarah asked her friends as Mia and Simone slowly walked over to join them. 'What do you think will happen here then?'

'Who knows?' Grace replied.

'We certainly don't,' Hannah said with a smile. 'We've been surprised by everything so far.'

Simone and Mia reached them and they stood up from the bench.

'Do you still want that hot chocolate?' Simone asked.

'Lead the way!' Grace replied.

The six girls walked down the driveway, with Abi, Hannah, Sarah and Grace pushing their bikes alongside them. Every Christmas Eve for forty years the Grainger house had stood on its own, empty, cold and quiet. Now the girls' voices fluttered about with the snowflakes, covering everything with a new layer of life.

Acknowledgements

I would like to send a very special thank-you to the young readers who let me know how much they enjoyed *The Lost Bride*, in particular Noah McCarthy Dunne, Kate O'Reilly, Catherine Simms, Iseult Law, Ruth McGahon, Áine Cassidy and Millie Kennedy. It's wonderful to have your support and enthusiasm!

I would like to thank my editors at Puffin: Lindsey Heaven, Wendy Shakespeare and Jennie Roman. In Puffin's Irish office I would particularly like to thank Patricia McVeigh for her great support and for managing to make promotional work fun. Thanks also to Phil Twomey. A special thanks to Paddy O'Doherty for her role in bringing this series into being in the first place. Many thanks to Faith O'Grady for her support and advice. A special mention for Erris, Meeda and Conne. And thank you, Donagh, for plot discussions in Amsterdam!

It all started with a Scarecrow.

Puffin is seventy years old.
Sounds ancient, doesn't it? But Puffin has never been
so lively. We're always on the lookout for the next big
idea, which is how it began all those years ago.

Penguin Books was a big idea from the mind of
a man called Allen Lane, who in 1935 invented
the quality paperback and changed the world.
**And from great Penguins, great Puffins grew,
changing the face of children's books forever.**

The first four Puffin Picture Books were hatched in 1940 and the
first Puffin story book featured a man with broomstick arms called
Worzel Gummidge. In 1967 Kaye Webb, Puffin Editor, started the
Puffin Club, promising to **'make children into readers'**.
She kept that promise and over 200,000 children became
devoted Puffineers through their quarterly instalments of
Puffin Post, which is now back for a new generation.

Many years from now, we hope you'll look back and
remember Puffin with a smile. **No matter what your age
or what you're into, there's a Puffin for everyone.**
The possibilities are endless, but one thing is for sure:
whether it's a picture book or a paperback, a sticker book
or a hardback, **if it's got that little Puffin
on it – it's bound to be good.**

Bright and shiny and sizzling with fun stuff . . .

puffin.co.uk

WEB FUN

UNIQUE and exclusive digital content!
Podcasts, photos, Q&A, Day in the Life of, interviews
and much more, from Eoin Colfer, Cathy Cassidy,
Allan Ahlberg and Meg Rosoff to Lynley Dodd!

WEB NEWS

The **Puffin Blog** is packed with posts and photos from
Puffin HQ and special guest bloggers. You can also sign up
to our monthly newsletter **Puffin Beak Speak**

WEB CHAT

Discover something new EVERY month –
books, competitions and treats galore

WEBBED FEET

(Puffins have funny little feet and
brightly coloured beaks)

Point your mouse our way today!